FOR RON,

My Muse

FOR WHERE YOUR
TREASURE IS, THERE YOUR
HEART WILL BE ALSO.

Mathew 6:21

LAND GRAB

KIT KARSON

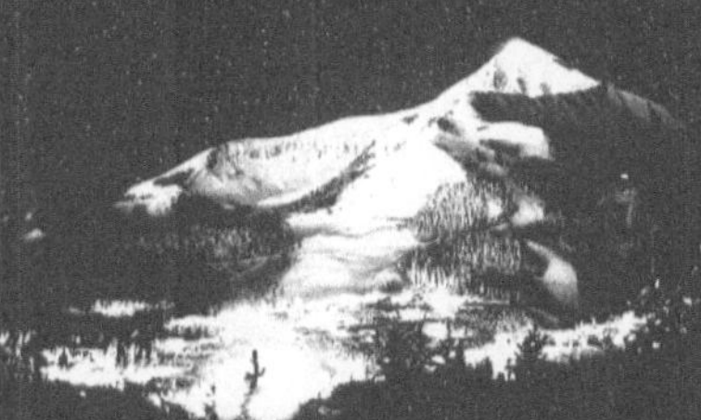

Book design by Colleen Sheehan

ISBN 979-8-9873287-0-5 (hard cover)
ISBN 979-8-9873287-1-2 (paperback)
ISBN 979-8-9873287-2-9 (ebook)
ISBN 979-8-9873287-3-6 (audiobook)

OLD-TIMERS STILL TALK, as old-timers do, about how the little town used to be, before the brewery, and the sapphire hunters, and the moneyed outsiders looking for their own private mountain getaway. In the before days, bars and churches vied for top billing. A grocery store anchored one corner of Main Street, balanced by a feed store on the other. A clothing store, doctor's office and pharmacy stair stepped up the mountain on one side of the street, opposite a car dealership and hardware store. Instead of tourists, the streets bustled with local ranchers and their families going about the business of life in a dusty cow town. Then came the sapphires.

Sapphires. Rarer than diamonds, and some would argue, more desirable. Formed from the slow cooling of molten rock and magma deep under the surface of the earth. During a different age, when the earth's crust was unstable and magma boiled and lava flowed, the colorless mineral corundum blended with other minerals to form prized crystals in a variety of colors. Sapphires. The most coveted of these, a mixture of corundum, titanium, and iron resulted in shades of blue. Sapphires flowed to the surface of the earth on rivers of magma which, when cooled, became granite. So precise are the chemical and physical requirements in the formation of sapphires that few places on earth have yielded these crystals. Trained geologists search in vain for the volcanic source of the sapphires found in Stone County Montana. For some treasures there is not an earthly explanation.

Unlike most western towns, Anderson began as a ranch outpost. The landowner held high standards in regard to behavior, and that attitude held through the many decades. Anderson residents, many with deep roots tracing back to the original family, prided themselves on a high code of ethics. Crime was low among locals and most disagreements could be solved with a few phone calls from the sheriff's office.

Peter Elliott sat looking out the window of his spacious office in the historic courthouse of the lively little town. His town. As sheriff of Anderson, Montana, he felt more than a small amount of pride over the quaint and pretty place. Tucked up against the Moonlight Mountains in southwest Montana, Anderson was nestled in pine covered slopes, its base washed in the deep pools and river rock covered stream beds of Flint Creek. Anderson was as beautiful as it was charming. Many old mining towns, behind the brick façade of the grand Main Street buildings, were scattered with decaying shacks and piles of 'historic' garbage. Anderson's Historical Society had a tendency to swoon every time a gardener turned up a rusted tin can or brown glass tincture bottle. Often the town council had to intervene when the Society, as it was locally known, tried to declare a resident's backyard an historical landmark and rope it off for further research. The elders of Anderson had the foresight to tear down and clear what could not be saved and preserve what could before the Society arrived to shut down any progress in that department. Left was a tidy town with minimal decay and room to grow where the lots of rubble were cleared.

Treasure hunters in days gone by came to Anderson in search of wealth in the form of silver and gold. Modern day treasure hunters are parents and their children hunting sapphires and a day's entertainment. The Sapphire Pit offered that opportunity. With the window open to let in fresh mountain air, Peter heard rather than saw a commotion at The

Sapphire Pit. Sliding the paperback he was reading under the pile of paperwork he was avoiding; Peter stood, smoothed his unruly mahogany hair with one hand and donned his required Stetson with the other. Early in his career he learned that tourists, if not locals, gave him more credence as a small-town western sheriff if he looked the part. He walked to the window and studied the sorting lot located at the bottom of a steep hill, directly below his window. There was indeed a group of angry customers on the verge of an altercation. Peter sighed. At times he felt more like a school principal than a law enforcement officer.

Peter took advantage of any excuse to go outside and enjoy the summer sunshine. He whistled to his dog, Zack, and slipped through one of the most protected secrets in Anderson, the back entrance to the sheriff's office. Hearsay, passed down from sheriff to sheriff, was that the entrance had not been in the original plans for the old courthouse, but was a special request from the residing sheriff. Regardless, it came in handy when avoiding a visit from an annoying councilman or an irate citizen. It was also a shortcut down the hill where he was headed to break up the latest playground fight.

When Peter reached the sorting lot, he saw David Howard, local patriarch, amid the ruckus. David, a weathered octogenarian and uncle to the owner, often volunteered his time on sapphire tours. In exchange for a free lunch and bucket of soil, he rode the tourist bus up the steep forested mountain road to the local sapphire mine. Once there, he gave a lecture on sapphire mining and how to find sapphires in a bucket of dirt. Each of the tourists was allowed to fill a bucket, which was then brought back to town for sorting.

David was, at the moment, being berated by an irate soccer mom.

"If Billy said you took his stone," she yelled, "then you took his stone. Give it back!"

David's mood was fast changing from bewildered to angry as he tried to protect his shins from an obese blond kid kicking furiously while screaming "Mine, mine, mine!"

Peter walked in and yelled, "Stop!"

His deep booming voice combined with his six-foot-five, 200-pound frame of lean muscle was hard to ignore. Even the boy stopped mid-tantrum to stare open mouthed at the large cowboy with the star pinned to his shirt. An added touch was the giant male German shepherd at his side.

"What is the problem here?" asked Peter.

"This man stole my Billy's sapphire," said the mom as Billy began his "mine, mine, mine!" chant in rhythm with accompanying kicks to David's shins.

Peter once again yelled, "Stop! If you kick him one more time, young man, I will throw you in jail."

Billy gave Peter a frightened look and hid behind his angry mother.

"David," said Peter, "you tell me your side of the story."

"I was sorting through my bucket and found a really nice stone," said David. "I was holding it up to the light and rubbing the dirt off and this kid started yelling that it was his."

Holly Noelle, owner of The Sapphire Pit, brushed a stray strand of tightly curled brown hair from her dirt smudged face.

"Sheriff," said Holly, "that kid and his mom have their buckets on the other side of the lot. Uncle Dave has been sitting here sorting his bucket since we came down from the mountain."

A young man at an adjoining table said, "And that kid has been nothing but trouble since he got on the bus. He ate his own lunch and then accused the guy in the next seat of stealing it. Holly gave him her lunch just to shut him up."

Sorters at the other tables nodded and murmured in agreement.

"Ma'am," said Peter to the mom in his well-practiced, soothing public servant voice, "I don't see how that stone could possibly belong to your son."

"Are you calling my son a liar?"

"At the very least he is confused. I suggest you and your son sit quietly and finish sorting your buckets or take them home to sort."

"I want my money back. This is a racket," said the mom, although her nervous glances from Zack to Peter belied her bluster. "I'll bet they sort all the big sapphires out of that dirt before they let us dig. They owe us!"

"Ma'am, you participated in the bus ride. You ate the lunch, plus an extra. You listened to the training lecture and have your buckets of dirt," said Peter. "There is nothing that you were promised that you have not received. Collect your belongings and I will walk you to your vehicle."

Sensing no support for her cause, but continuing to mutter under her breath, the mother grabbed Billy's arm and half-drug him across the lot to their table where she collected backpack and purse, sunhats, water bottles, and the rest of the paraphernalia involved in a day in the sun. Peter was not surprised to see a timid and cowed looking man standing next to the table, scooping dirt back into buckets. The man picked up the buckets and trotted after the woman without a word. Noting the Missoula license plates, Peter watched as the family loaded their minivan with themselves and their belongings. He placed his hands on the rim of the car window as they prepared to drive away, looked sternly into the woman's eyes, and said, "Consider going elsewhere on your next family outing. You are no longer welcome in Anderson."

Returning to a chorus of cheers and clapping, Peter tipped his hat to the sapphire hunters. While Holly and David thanked Peter profusely for his help, Zack made his way around the lot, tail wagging, greeting each guest and begging for pats. Gone was any illusion of a vicious beast. Across the lot, a heavily made-up woman with eyes like a hunter, sashayed her way toward Peter. Liz Benton. He turned and escaped to the boardwalk before he could get caught in her trap.

Peter glanced in each direction along the wooden sidewalk running most of the length on both sides of Main Street. Much time was spent maintaining the boardwalks while preserving an illusion of rustic authenticity. Few tourists suspected decaying concrete sidewalks were hidden beneath the weathered wooden boards. In contrast, colorfully painted late Victorian era houses dressed in towers and turrets rubbed shoulders with stately red brick professional buildings. Peter paused for a moment, enjoying the beauty of his surroundings. To the south, Empire Peak was etched with ski runs and snow cover even in late spring. The Moonlight Mountains, rife with beauty and mystery, reigned over the east. Flint

Creek and the valley it nourished opened out to the north and west.

Irresistible aromas of baked goods wafted through the air from the bakery next door to The Sapphire Pit. Giving into temptation, Peter stopped in for a mid-afternoon snack. Sally, the granddaughter of owners Bob and Barb Dahl, was manning the till. Sally's big blue eyes barely cleared the top of the display case, but she managed to see everything going on inside and outside the bakery and was in hot contention for the prize of most prolific gossip in town. What set Sally apart was her complete lack of malice. Those blue eyes, topped with a mop of curly blonde hair, were filled with pure love. A quarrel at the Sapphire Pit would have her calling her church prayer chain and planning a reconciliation potluck.

"Oh, my goodness, Sheriff Elliott, I hope everything's okay at the Sapphire Pit. All that yelling . . . should I send over a basket of goodies to sweeten tempers?"

Peter gave her a quick, watered-down version of the incident and assured her everything was fine. Sally, knowing Peter's weakness, handed him a freshly baked cinnamon roll in a go-box, flipped a sugar cookie to Zack, and sent them on their way, refusing Peter's attempt to pay. *Baked goods for information,* thought Peter. *I wonder if there is an ethics violation in that.*

Peter walked past the quilt shop next to the bakery, jumping when the door banged open.

"Don't you dare come into this shop with that!" yelled Margaret Franks, cantankerous owner of Prime Cuts, which, because of its name, was often mistaken for a butcher shop.

"I'm on my way to my office, Margaret. I'm not in need of quilting supplies today," said Peter.

"Don't be a smart aleck!" snapped Margaret, a tall bony woman with a perpetually discontented look. "When are you going to shut that place down?"

Margaret was referring to the bakery, for which she had an illogical hatred. Several years ago, someone came into her shop eating a gooey Danish and left sticky fingerprints on several pieces of material. Since then, Margaret had become militant about food and drink brought into her shop. The door and windows were posted with warnings, and security cameras guarded every nook and cranny. Margaret hadn't stopped there. She reported the bakery to the health department every several months. A health violation had never been found, but inspectors showed up periodically for baked goods and to check off the complaint box.

"There is no valid reason to shut down the bakery, Margaret," said Peter. "It is a clean, well-run business."

"Hrrumph. I'll get them someday," replied Margaret as she turned and stomped her way back into the shop, slamming the door behind her.

Peter shook his head and made a beeline for his office. Built at the highest point of town proper, the courthouse cast a stately shadow over its subjects. Wide stone steps led the way into the brick and granite building. Those granite walls isolated the interior from the noise and chaos outside. Inside, Peter inhaled the familiar scent of floor polish, and listened to the echoes of his footfalls. There was something comforting about the quiet peace of the building.

Waiting for him were his clerk and deputy, two people who, if matched stereotypes, would have been in opposite roles. His deputy, Helen Ferguson, was a fiftyish woman in a losing battle with a bulging waistline. Years ago, she gave up attempting to hide her age with hair dye and now wore her salt and pepper hair in a long braid. Travis, the clerk, was a twenty-six-year-old body builder. Travis originally signed up for the deputy position. Blond and buff, he wore his uniform well, but quickly realized he didn't have the temperament to be a deputy sheriff after his first call out to a domestic dispute. He tried to 'save' the wife of the disputing couple only to be cold cocked by the woman who was the aggressor in the situation.

Peter leaned against the antique oak filing cabinet in the outer office and filled them in on his afternoon activities.

"You know," said Travis, "Harold Evans is selling his gift shop."

"And...?" asked Peter.

"It would be a perfect place for Margaret to move her quilt shop. She would be sandwiched between a jewelry store and a clothing store. No more harassing the Dahls' bakery," said Travis.

"And there's more room," said Helen, eyeing Peter's cinnamon roll. "Margaret's always complaining about wanting to expand her shop and not having enough space."

Peter, eyeing Helen's already straining uniform buttons, slipped the roll behind his back.

"Good thought," said Peter. "I'll mention it to her. I'd love to hear the end of that squabble."

2

Liz benton had only one concern in life, and that concern was herself. She had a good job in a back office at the local bank dealing with numbers, and Liz was very good with numbers. The position required zero contact with customers and very little contact with coworkers, which was a blessing for everyone involved. Liz Benton was not a nice person. She had a few women she called friends who were little more than hangers-on left over from her days as head mean girl in high school. She had no interest in relationships with other people unless they could benefit her in some way. Recently, after too many rounds of beer at the brewery, and one of the rare times she actually paid attention to the chatter of her drinking buddies, she realized that they had all gotten married. Liz didn't bother with weddings and other events that diverted attention from herself, so, although these girls begged her to be a part of the festivities, she always found an excuse to be out of town. Usually, a fictitious relative died, and a funeral was occurring on the same date as the wedding. Anyone paying attention would have noticed she came back relaxed and refreshed from a week at a high-end spa. Liz wasn't so interested in the tales of romance or mortgages or babies, what caught her attention was the talk of paychecks and bonuses and exotic trips. Her three friends had found husbands. One left her job after marriage and now spent her days at the nail salon or sipping wine on the back deck of her new house. The other two still worked, but now their paychecks were spent on themselves. Liz realized she was missing out. She needed a husband. Liz began taking an inventory of eligible men in Anderson. She was more concerned with bank account balances than other factors such as age, but her vanity required a handsome man to flaunt. She had access to bank accounts and an eye for beauty. Months of investigation narrowed her choice to one, Peter Elliott. Unbeknownst to the rest of the town, Peter was a wealthy man. There was more in his bank account than should have been for a small-town sheriff. Liz didn't care where the money came from, it was there. Combined with luscious hair in a deep shade of mahogany and intense blue eyes, it was often said that Peter's smile could charm a rattlesnake out of its skin. He was sought after by more than one hopeful woman in town, and Liz planned on bagging her prey.

Liz was not a good neighbor. She played her music too loud and was noisy coming home from the bars in the wee hours of the morning. Rather than paying the monthly trash collection fee, she threw her garbage into her neighbor's bins. One sunny afternoon, Liz walked out her back door to throw trash into an alley dumpster and on her steps was a dirty, war-weary, tabby tomcat. The cat had no interest in human interaction. He had a sunny place to sit and lick his most recent wounds and Liz was invading his space. He hissed and spat and threatened to bite. Liz, most days, would have given him a swift kick across the yard, but, in a sudden Grinch-like growing of her small black heart, she felt a kinship for the nasty thing. If he were human, he would be a drinking buddy. To her own surprise, on her next trip to the grocery store, Liz found herself buying food for the cat.

Bob and Barb Dahl were neighbors, and they did not like Liz. She insisted on making noise after seven in the evening and the local police force ignored their complaints. They were sure Liz was the one who threw empty beer cans in their yard out of spite, but they had no proof.

One sunny day, as Barb was sitting on her back deck sipping gin and tonics, she glanced over and, to her amazement, saw Liz feeding an old, battered tomcat. Barb had a deep fondness for cats and, thus, for other cat lovers. She felt an immediate affinity for Liz and called over to her.

"Liz. Yoo hoo, Liz."

Liz, expecting an onslaught of complaints, was tempted to ignore Barb, but braced herself and turned around, ready with her own verbal assault. To her surprise, Barb waved her over.

"Come have a cool drink with me if you aren't busy. The deck is perfect this time of day," said Barb.

Liz, not one to turn down an offer of free alcohol, did just that. An unusual companionship was formed that day. There wasn't friendly chat or sharing of lives. They sat and drank and complained about imagined slights or city government, but mostly sat and drank. Occasionally, Bob would bring out his cookbooks and read recipes while they drank.

The afternoon of The Sapphire Pit incident, Liz stomped home fuming at the thought Peter may have snubbed her. Surely, he hadn't seen her walking across the lot, or he would have stayed to chat. What man could resist her after all? While in the backyard setting out food for the ratty old tomcat,

Liz noticed Bob sitting on the back deck by himself, reading a book.

"Where's Barb today?" she asked.

"Quilt show in Rumsey," said Bob. "But the gin is cold. Come over. I'll mix you a drink."

Bob, having been married to a petulant woman for almost forty years, could read the signs.

"Something bothering you today, Liz?"

Liz hesitated, but finally said, "Oh, a guy I thought I was interested in. I'm not sure he's interested in me."

"Ah."

A side effect of being a selfish, unsympathetic person is not receiving sympathy from other people. Sensing unfamiliar compassion from Bob, the dam broke, and Liz spilled out her frustrations.

"It's Peter Elliot. He would make a wonderful husband, but that Holly Noelle has some kind of weird hold on him!"

3

S LEEP CAME EASY, the awakening, not so much. Peter's body shuddered on being pulled out of a deep, dream-filled sleep by the obnoxious gong of his cell phone, purposely set that way so he wouldn't sleep through an important call. He looked at the time as he swiped to answer. 5:38 a.m.

"Yeah?" he said, his voice gravelly with sleep.

"Peter?"

"Yeah. Travis. What's up?"

"They need you down at the bakery ASAP. We've got a body."

Peter sat straight up in bed. Instantly on alert.

"What?! Who?" he asked.

"Bob Dahl. He left home early this morning to get the bread dough mixed and rising. Barb came in later and found him." Travis' voice cracked. "It's really bad, Pete."

"Where's Helen?"

"She's inside. She called me down to help out with Barb and keep the area secure."

"Call in Tom. I'll be there as soon as I can."

Peter hurried on with his clothes. Dead bodies were his least favorite part of the job. In a small town, too often the deceased was someone he knew.

He arrived on the scene to find, even at this early hour, a scattering of curious onlookers. Not for the first time, he wondered how news traveled so fast in the small community. His official police vehicle and lights helped clear a path to the front door.

"Stay here, Zack," said Peter.

He rolled down the windows before he opened the door and stepped out.

In spite of his sweet temperament, Zack was a well-disciplined, fully trained police dog. The trainer, a friend of Peter's from Chicago, shipped Zack to Anderson when it became obvious he didn't have the aggressiveness needed for a big city police force.

Short and stout Tom Edwards, part-time deputy, was there, and already had the sidewalk in front of the bakery roped off.

"Hey Pete," said Tom, "area secured. Barb is in the back of my vehicle. I thought she could use some privacy. Sally's in Missoula visiting friends. Barb's going to call her. Helen is inside."

"Thanks, Tom. Stay out here and keep the crowd in line," said Peter.

He saw Travis standing next to the building looking slightly queasy and took pity on him.

"Travis," said Peter, "go on back to the office and man the phones. 'No comment' on everything."

"Thanks, Boss. Should I get food and coffee sent down? You guys will be here for a while."

"Thanks, but it looks like it's already been taken care of."

Linda Elliott, head of the Christian Women's Society and Peter's sister-in-law, was on her way down the sidewalk pulling a jumbo green garden wagon laden with two large hot-drink dispensers and boxes of what he assumed was food.

"Peter," she called, "I have hot tea and coffee and breakfast food for you folks."

Baptist women are amazing, thought Peter. They seemed to have an endless supply of food and drink ready and waiting for any occasion. And he was especially thankful for Linda. She knew that Peter, unlike most cops, despised coffee. He likened the taste to sewer water and a small sip would leave him with his head in the toilet puking for the rest of the day.

"Thank you, Linda," said Peter as he felt rather than heard his stomach growling. "You have no idea how much we appreciate you."

"Likewise, Sheriff, we're happy to help. Just get the dispensers and utensils back when you get a chance. No hurry."

Wanting nothing less than to dig into the boxes of food and pour a hot cup of tea, Peter squashed his hunger and steeled himself to what was awaiting him inside. Helen met him at the door wearing full crime scene protective equipment: black jumpsuit, hairnet, face shield, gloves, and booties. She handed him a set of his own and stood by until she made sure he had every piece in place.

"All this for a dead body?" asked Peter.

"Expect the worst," was all Helen said as she stepped aside so he could enter.

The outer room of the bakery was deserted and dark, lit only by the glow from streetlights. The display cases, as usual, had been emptied the night before, ready to be filled with fresh baked goods in the morning. Helen pointed him toward what he knew was a kitchen in the back. As Peter walked in, he smelled the coppery scent of blood, but it didn't prepare him for what he saw.

What had been a sterile white-tiled and stainless-steel industrial kitchen, was now a room of horror. Blood was splattered across walls and dripping from the ceiling. After the initial shock passed, Peter looked around the room. His eyes stopped at a stocking clad foot sticking out of the giant bowl of an industrial sized dough mixer. Bob.

"It was still mixing when I got here," said Helen. "I found the fuse box behind the door. Thank goodness the fuse for the mixer was clearly marked."

Helen and Peter stared at each other, both with a mix of shock and revulsion on their faces.

"I didn't have the nerve to look in the bowl," said Helen.

Peter walked over to the mixer, Helen at his side. They peered over the edge of the bowl. Staring back at them from the bottom of the bowl were a pair of lifeless green eyes.

"That's not Bob," said Helen.

Bob Dahl, like Sally, had big blue eyes in a soft chubby face. The green-eyed face in the mixer bowl was thin and weathered.

"That's Sam Geary, the dairy man," said Peter.

"What on earth could have happened?" asked Helen. "And where's Bob?"

"No idea. Sam would have been here early this morning delivering milk and butter. I wonder what he walked into."

As they were standing looking at the lifeless, blood-encrusted face of Sam Geary, the contents of the bowl shifted, and the sentinel leg leaned, then flipped out onto the floor, splattering them both with blood.

"Okay," said Helen. "I didn't need to see that."

Peter didn't say anything. Helen, having grown up on a nearby cattle ranch, learned from a young age how to butcher anything from a cow to elk and deer during hunting season. She seemed immune to an occasional mutilated human body. Peter didn't want to admit that if something bothered Helen, it would give him nightmares.

He pulled out his phone and punched in the number for Travis.

"Hey, Travis. Would you call Dr. Hamm? I'd like him to look at the body before we take it out of the bowl and then do an autopsy this morning if possible."

"Sure," said Travis. "He's usually up and working out by now. If he doesn't answer, I'll drive over."

Although in his mid-sixties, Dr. Hamm still entered, and won, body building contests. Movie star handsome, with silver hair and twinkling blue-green eyes, he would have been the most sought-after male in town if his complete devotion to his wife wasn't well-known.

"Did anyone look in the alley?" Peter asked Helen.

"Not yet."

"Okay. I'll go around the front, so we don't con-taminate the crime scene. We need to work on the assumption this was murder."

"No kidding," muttered Helen, already walking out the door to grab her kit.

Thanks to a wealthy benefactor, who was also a fan of forensic dramas, Stone County had a seemingly endless training and forensic equipment budget. Peter, Helen, and Tom went to every available class. Travis reserved his training for anything not involving gore. Helen, out of them all, had a particularly strong aptitude for forensics.

Peter left through the front door and walked around the building to the alley. Parked by the bakery's back door, motor still running and refrigerator compartment wide open, was Sam Geary's delivery truck. Peter stepped into the cab and turned the key off. He walked to the front and into the building, poking his head through the kitchen doorway.

"Helen, Sam's delivery truck is out back. I turned it off but left everything else untouched."

"Okay, Boss. I'll work it up when I'm done here. Can someone keep an eye on things back there?"

"Yeah, I'll have Tom rope it off."

Peter made his way to Linda's breakfast wagon. He poured one cup each of hot coffee and tea and grabbed a bag of Danish pastries before walking over to Tom's Ford Explorer where Barb Dahl was waiting. He opened the rear door and climbed in next to her. She was beyond sobbing and stared blankly out the window.

"Hey, Barb," said Peter, handing her the coffee and a sweet roll.

"Peter," said Barb, anguish cracking her voice.

Peter put his arm around her shoulder and gave her a comforting hug.

"Barb, the body in the mixer isn't Bob."

"What?!" said Barb, looking at Peter in disbelief.

"It's Sam Geary."

"The dairy man?"

"Yes. Barb, I need to ask you some questions about this morning. I know it's hard, but we have to figure out what happened here. Would it be more comfortable for you if we did this here or down at the station?"

"But where's Bob?" said Barb, sobbing again.

"I don't know, but we need to start looking for him as soon as possible. The more we know, the better chance we have of finding him."

"I don't know anything," she said. "He left for work this morning. I haven't heard from him since."

"Do you mind if I tape this?" asked Peter. "Just so I don't overlook anything important."

"I don't mind. Anything that will help bring Bob back."

Peter pulled a small tape recorder out of his left shirt pocket and set it on the bench seat between them.

"Was there anything unusual about this morning? A change in Bob's routine?"

"No, not at all. He gets up at the same time every morning, except Sundays. We're closed on the Sabbath."

"What time does he get up?"

"At three-thirty and leaves around four. He opens the bakery, turns on all the equipment, and takes out the ingredients for baking. Some things like eggs and butter and milk need to warm up to room temperature."

"What about Sam Geary? When does he usually show up?"

"Before I get there. Between four and five."

"And you go in around five?"

"Yes."

"Tell me about this morning."

"I went in at the usual time."

"At five?"

"It might have been a few minutes after. It's not like I have to clock in," said Barb defensively.

"I'm not concerned with you being late for work, Barb. I need to know the times for the murder investigation."

"It was probably about a quarter after five."

"Did you go in the back door or the front door?"

"The front. I don't like using the alley entrance, especially in the morning. It's too dark and hard to walk in the gravel."

"Did you notice anything different this morning?"

Barb coughed and sobbed and stifled a gag. "The smell . . . it was sooo bad. And then the blood. So much blood."

"What did you do?"

"I ran out the door. I was screaming and screaming, and nobody would help me. Then the deputy came."

"Tom?"

"No, the young one."

"Travis?"

"Yes. He let me sit in his car until the grocery clerk came."

Good grief, I don't know if she's being rude or oblivious, thought Peter. He didn't correct her that Travis was the clerk in the sheriff's office and Tom was an official deputy.

"Was Bob having problems of any kind? Was there any reason someone would want to hurt him?"

Peter noticed a momentary hesitation before Barb answered.

"No. Nothing."

"Are you certain?" asked Peter, closely watching her expression.

"Nothing," said Barb, her face a mask.

"Was there anything unusual going on with Sam Geary? Did he and Bob have any issues?"

"No. Sam is . . . was a good guy. No issues."

"Okay. One more thing, I'll need something of Bob's, a piece of clothing. Zack may be able to pick up a scent trail."

Peter saw Dr. Hamm arrive in his white Dodge Ram truck.

"Barb," he said. "I'm going to ask Dr. Hamm to give you a sedative to help you rest. Is there someone who can stay with you?"

"Linda could stay for a while. I know she wouldn't mind."

"Okay. I'll give her a call while you're talking to Dr. Hamm. Tom can give you a ride home when you're ready and also pick up that piece of clothing."

"What about my car?"

"Oh," said Peter. "I guess you would have a car here. Are you okay to drive yourself home?"

"Yeah, I'm good. It's just a few blocks. I'll walk down and pick up Bob's car later."

Peter looked at her, surprised. "Bob's car is here?"

"In the side parking lot next to mine," said Barb, pointing to a faded red Ford Taurus parked next to a newer orange Nissan Rogue.

"Which one is Bob's?" asked Peter.

"The Taurus."

"Is it okay if we search it? There may be a clue to where he went."

"Sure. He never locks it. The keys are probably in the ignition. Bring it home when you're done."

Peter climbed out of the Explorer and approached the doctor.

"Hey, Doc," said Peter. "Sorry to get you out this early."

"No worries, Peter. I was already up."

"Did Travis fill you in on the situation?"

"He did. Bob Dahl murdered. Sad."

"Uh, no," said Peter. "It isn't Bob. It's Sam Geary."

Dr. Hamm gave him a puzzled look.

"Travis confused?" he asked.

"No," said Peter. "I guess we haven't updated Travis. Say, Barb is over there in Tom's Explorer. Could you have a look at her before she goes home? She's pretty upset. When you're finished, Helen is in the bakery processing the scene. She'll fill you in."

Peter walked back to his own vehicle, drove to the edge of town, and steeled himself for his next unpleasant task, informing the newly widowed Mrs. Geary of her husband's gruesome death. Flashbacks of the Stone County sheriff of days gone by standing at the door to inform him and his brother of their parents' death haunted him. He prayed he would get to the Gearys before one of the sidewalk busybodies caught wind of the body ID and took it upon themselves to break the news.

The Geary place sat north of Anderson, where hills retreated and the valley opened on both sides of Flint Creek, resulting in wide fertile fields for growing the variety of grains and grasses needed for plentiful, rich milk production. Milking parlors and equipment sheds were tucked in hollows behind the surrounding hills, leaving the open areas for farming. As an unintended result, the beauty of the valley from a roadside perspective was retained. A massive stone and log house perched atop a hillside overlooked Geary lands, keeping a watchful eye on the empire. Mrs. Geary, stooped and arthritic from a lifetime of hard work, watched the sheriff's vehicle make its way up the meandering driveway, expecting nothing more than a report of cows on the road. She opened the door before the doorbell finished chiming.

"Good morning, Sheriff. To what do I owe this pleasure?"

"Good morning, Mrs. Geary," said Peter, removing his Stetson and holding it respectfully at his side.

"Enough of this Mrs. Geary nonsense. I've known you since you were born, Peter. Call me Mary. Come in and have a cup of coffee," she said as she turned and shuffled into the depth of the house. She glanced back to make sure he was following. "I baked a nice coffee cake this morning. It should be cool enough to slice by now. Bring that dog in with you. I'm sure he'd like a piece of coffee cake, too."

Peter followed obediently, dreading the conversation to come.

"Any of the family around today Mrs … ummm … I mean Mary?" he asked.

"Oh, they're all out playing with the cows. I rarely see them unless they're hungry."

Mary sliced three large pieces of coffee cake, placing two on plates and one in an old pie tin she set on the floor.

"I do miss having a dog around," said Mary

The kitchen smelled of cinnamon and melted butter, making Peter's stomach growl. He felt guilty for being hungry when Sam Geary was dead, and his family didn't know.

"It is possible to call them to the house? I need to talk to you all about something important."

"Sit first," she said as she set the plates on an oversized rustic plank table. "They all have those cell phones now. I'll call and ask them to come in. If it's just cows on the road, I can tell them over the phone."

"It's not about cows," said Peter quietly, to her retreating back.

"All set." She walked back into the kitchen. "They're just about done feeding and said they'd come in after that."

Peter ate his coffee cake and did his best to keep up with Mary's chatter while they waited.

He heard a screen door squeak open and then slap shut accompanied by the heavy thump of work boots. Seth Geary, the eldest son of Sam and Mary, stalked into the room with a scowl on his face.

"That watering hole is ours dead to rights, Sheriff. Winston Hayes can't take back a property boundary that's been held for over a hundred years."

Peter, with a well-honed poker face, set that statement aside for future inquiry.

"I'm not here about a property dispute, Seth."

The screen door once again squeaked, and more boots clomped into the room. One-by-one Mary's three children and their spouses gathered in the kitchen, faces a muddy mix of curiosity and concern.

"You know all the family, don't you Peter?" asked Mary.

"Seth, I know," said Peter, standing to greet the family. "I don't think I've met the younger siblings."

"Seth's wife Hannah is in town today," said Mary, "but everyone else is here."

A much younger version of Mary stepped forward, shifting a toddler from her right hip to her left so she could reach out her hand to Peter.

"I'm Beth and this is my husband, Matthew." She gazed fondly at the babe in her arms. "And this is Joey."

"I'm Seth and Beth's baby brother, Andrew," said a young man who favored his father's side of the family. "This is my wife, Michelle."

A pretty girl with a brown pixie cut stepped forward.

"Pleased to meet you, Sheriff," she said, holding out her hand.

"So, what's this all about then, Sheriff?" asked Seth, impatient with the formalities. "Dad's not back from town, but everyone else is here."

Peter, hat in hand, took a deep breath and cleared his throat.

"Your dad was killed in town this morning. He won't be coming home. I'm so sorry."

Mary brought her hands to her face, her already bent body crumpling, and wailed.

The room was filled with gasps and moans and disbelief.

Seth, head of the family by default, led his stunned sister to Peter's vacated chair.

"Please tell us what happened to our father, Peter," said Andrew, the first to find his voice.

Peter relayed the horror of Sam's death.

"I don't understand," said Mary. "How did he fall into a mixer? It doesn't make sense."

"We'll know more after the autopsy, Mary. Dr. Hamm is working on that."

Peter hesitated, searching his brain for murder investigation protocol and hoping his inexperienced staff could handle what they had ahead of them.

"I need to question each of you individually," he said to the group.

"You think one of us had something to do with this?" said Beth.

"I'm looking for clues, Beth. One of you may have a thought or memory that could lead us in the right direction. Hearing each perspective individually will give me a clearer overall picture."

Mary nodded in understanding.

"You can use the office," she said, pointing toward an open doorway off the kitchen.

Peter gently questioned each member of the family. They were consistent in their answers: Yes, Sam had left on his regular time and delivery route. No, there was no reason anyone would want to hurt him. No, he hadn't seemed worried about anything, nor had he been acting strangely.

Peter saved Seth for last, sensing in his attitude deeper issues. The rest of the family trailed away to an inner room, milk and cows forgotten, death taking top billing in the hierarchy of life necessities.

Seth, scowl in place, studied his hands, calloused and soiled from a morning of hard work. He walked to the kitchen sink, turned on the hot water and scrubbed until Peter was sure the first few layers of skin must be gone. Seth dried his hands on a kitchen towel, turned to the coffee pot and unhooked a large mug off a wall-mounted rack. The rack was all too familiar to Peter. Worn and discarded horseshoes are part of the routine clutter of life on a ranch. Sam Geary, ever frugal, saved every old horseshoe that hit the ground since he was around twelve and made them into useful things. There weren't many houses in Anderson without a horseshoe coffee mug rack mounted to the wall next to the coffee pot. Seth filled his mug, pulled out the recently vacated kitchen chair next to Peter and sat with a sigh. Zack moved from his place at Peter's side and laid his head in Seth's lap.

"I don't get it, Peter," said Seth, fondling Zack's ears. "How did this happen?"

"We're not sure, Seth. There are a lot of unanswered questions. Dr. Hamm will do an autopsy. That may help us determine if Sam was attacked or somehow fell into the mixing bowl."

"And you said Bob Dahl is missing?"

"He is. Barb came in late and saw the blood and the body, and assumed it was Bob. We have no idea what happened to Bob."

"Do you think Bob attacked Dad?"

"We don't know if Bob attacked your dad. Bob's car is still parked outside the bakery. If he took off, it wasn't in his car. Did your dad ever have any problems with the Dahls? Any business disagreements?"

"Not so much disagreements. Bob was at least six months late paying on invoices. Dad didn't want to cut them off, so he traded them dairy for baked goods to cover some of the debt." Seth studied the many chairs spaced around the massive oak table. "It takes a lot of bread and cinnamon rolls to keep a family this size fed."

"But that didn't cover all he owed?"

"No. Dad was going to tell Bob he couldn't do business with him anymore. It would have been a blow to Bob. He couldn't get better prices anywhere else and nowhere else would give him credit."

"Okay, when you came in earlier, you mentioned a land dispute. Could you tell me about that?"

Seth took a slow sip of his coffee, set down the mug, and settled in for a telling.

"You know the old Murphy ranch? The one that borders us to the north?"

"Sure."

"There's a creek running through and a watering hole at the edge of the property. The story goes that a hundred and fifty odd years ago, when our great-granddads were all starting out, the Gearys and the Murphys came from Ireland and then by railroad to homestead here in Stone County. They chose neighboring homesteads, both with good grass and plenty of year-round water for cattle. That was a big deal back when swindlers were bringing folks out in the spring when everything was green and seasonal springs flowed. By midsummer the water was gone, and the grass was dead, but it was too late. Those folks had already sunk everything they had into those dream acres. I don't know if it was on purpose or accident, but the survey markers were set wrong, and my great-granddad was led to believe part of the creek was on his homestead. He chose this place and built his fence believing those markers. When surveyors came through and marked out the official boundaries, all that water was inside the Murphys' place. They had plenty of water including the rest of the creek, so they let the fence stay where it was and never a word was spoken about it until the last of the Murphys died off this spring. When the place was sold to Mr. Winston Hayes, he brought in surveyors who marked off the original boundaries, including the piece of creek. Mr. Hayes is demanding we move the fence."

"I believe that state laws would be on your side, Seth. After a certain amount of time, if a fence is agreed to by both parties, it would be recognized as a legal boundary."

"That's what I tried to tell him."

Seth looked toward the door and scooted his chair closer to Peter, lowering his voice to a whisper.

"The rest of the family doesn't know about this. Dad didn't want to worry them."

"Why do you think they would be worried?"

"We've been getting threatening letters and phone calls."

"From Winston Hayes?"

"Well . . . the letters aren't signed, and no names are said on the phone, but who else would it be?"

"Whose phone do the calls come to?"

"Dad's. I haven't heard them, just what he told me."

"Did he tell you what the caller says?"

"All threats. *'We're going to destroy your business and your family.'* That sort of thing."

"And you or your dad never thought to report this to the sheriff's office?"

"Dad didn't take it seriously. He thought it was kids making prank calls."

Peter couldn't help but roll his eyes. He took a small notebook and attached pencil out of the back pocket of his jeans.

"Can you give me his number? We may be able to trace the source of those calls."

Seth rattled Sam's phone number.

"Tell me about the letters. Are they sent through the mail?" asked Peter.

"No. They show up on Dad's delivery truck seat when he's in town. He'll go into a business and come back out and there it is."

"Any particular business?"

"No, different ones each time . . . like whoever is doing it knows his route."

"Or follows him. Do you have these letters?"

Seth checked the doorway again. "Yeah, but not here. At my house."

"I need to see them."

"Hold on."

Seth got up and walked into the living room. Finding no one there, he checked the rest of the house. He found the family in the backyard surrounded by rose bushes, Sam's pride and joy. "I smell cows all day," he would say. "I want to smell something pretty at night."

Seth walked back into the kitchen, motioning Peter to follow him out the door, through the squeaking screen. Peter whistled to Zack and followed. Seth had a house out of sight over the hill, but within walking distance of Mary and Sam's.

"I have them hidden in the garage," he said.

The path to Seth's house had grown through the years from a game trail to a rustic sidewalk. Early in their marriage, when the house was newly built, Seth and his wife Hannah widened and leveled the trail. They lined it with large river stones and filled-in gravel, and then sand. Every year, each child made a cement handprint steppingstone and placed it along the path. Sam built a bench at the crest of the hill, open on both sides for watching either the sunset or sunrise. Through the years, various family members planted wildflowers and roses and lilac bushes amongst the native grasses. Birdhouses, school and 4-H projects, were mounted on poles, carefully nailed together and painted in bright colors by the hands of children.

Reflections of a family filled with love, thought Peter, *and now torn apart by hate and greed.*

Over the hillcrest in a hidden meadow stood a rambling log house, barns and stables in a distant side yard and a garage close behind. Children's bikes and toys and playhouses filled the front yard. Peter took in the sight and his heart ached for the children who would soon hear the news of their beloved grandfather's death. An old yellow dog of indeterminate breeding snoozed on the front porch. He lifted his ears and thumped his tail in greeting to Zack but made no effort to move from his sunny spot. Chickens in a variety of colors and breeds pecked for bugs, equally oblivious to human events. Seth led Peter to the garage, unlocking the door with a key retrieved from the front pocket of his grubby jeans.

"You keep the door locked?"

"I do now, with the threats and everything going on."

"What else is going on, Seth?"

"I'll show you the letters."

Seth walked to a workbench on the far side of the garage. He lifted an old rusted and dented aluminum coffee can off the bench. With a twist of his hand, he removed the bottom and pulled out a wad of folded white business sized envelopes. He saw Peter's surprised look, grinned, and tipped the can forward so Peter could see the upper section of the can filled with an assortment of screws, nuts, and bolts.

"The old coffee can where used nuts and bolts go to die," said Seth. "Nobody will ever use them, but nobody wants to be the wasteful person who throws them away."

"Clever hideout."

"When we first got married, I was hooked on chewing tobacco. Hannah said she wouldn't marry me unless I quit. Making the promise was easy, shaking off the addiction not so much. It took a while. This is where I hid my cans of snoose until I kicked the habit completely."

Peter understood. Alcohol and tobacco were a way of life in rural ranching communities. Boys, especially, started when they were kids and were addicted by the time they were teenagers.

Seth handed him the letters. Peter reached out to take them and then thought better and reached into his pocket instead for the ever-present pair of purple nitrile gloves. After donning the gloves, he took the letters from Seth.

"Has anyone else touched these?"

"Just me, Dad, and whoever wrote them."

"Okay, good."

Black greasy fingerprints dotted the envelopes.

"Did you get them this way?" asked Peter.

"No," said Seth, sheepishly. "I was working on the tractor when Dad handed them to me. All the grease prints are mine."

"Good to know."

Careful not to smear the grease further, he studied the envelope. Other than the obvious smudges, there were no marks, no writing. The flaps were of the sort that had to be licked to seal and Peter wondered how backed up the state DNA lab was and if it would be worth sending in the envelope. DNA was worthless without a suspect DNA to compare. He opened the flap of the first envelope and pulled out a piece of paper torn from an old-fashioned composition notebook. One sentence filled the page in a large irregular scrawl.

> *You took what was mine and*
> *I'll take what is yours*

A chill ran down Peter's neck. "I can see why you lock the garage. Are the rest like this?"

"They get worse."

"How often did these show up?"

"About once a week, first a phone call in the night and the next morning there would be a letter on the truck seat."

"Any particular day?"

"Not that I noticed."

"What else are you doing for protection?"

"I bought two Great Pyrenees dogs. They're guarding the cows day and night."

An image of the old mutt sleeping on the front porch passed through Peter's mind.

"What about your family, Seth?"

"Everything I can, Peter, but it's hard when Dad won't let me tell anyone about the threats. I did tell Hannah, of course. We have a new German shepherd puppy who stays in the house at night. He's at the vet with Hannah getting his shots today. We've always had guns around, but now they're loaded and strategically placed around the house. Hannah has never been a shooter, but I got her a 12-gauge shotgun and a 9-mm pistol, and she practices at least once a week. The kids don't know why we're getting new dogs and new guns. Kids are just excited about a puppy; they don't ask why."

"And your mom and dad? Your mom said they haven't had a dog for a long time."

"More of my frustration. Mom doesn't know about the threats, but she'll have to be told now. She thinks she's too old to get a new dog. Dad at least let me put motion sensor security lights in their yard."

"Does she have a gun?"

Seth nodded. "And knows how to use it."

"I need to take these letters with me."

"Sure, Peter."

Seth locked the door behind them, and they made their way back up the path to the main ranch house. Mary was waiting for them on the front porch.

"I'm ready to see Sam now, Peter."

Peter put on his neutral face, not wanting this strong and noble women to see his pity.

"Not yet, Mary. Let us finish the investigation. I'll give you a call when the body, Sam, is ready."

Mary swallowed and nodded.

"You know best, Peter," she said as she turned and walked back into the house.

4

IN STONE COUNTY, the sheriff and coroner are dually elected, giving Peter the responsibilities of both offices. Bodies were found in the county periodically, but those situations were generally bland compared to what he found in the Sweet Dahl-ites bakery that morning. While Helen collected evidence at the crime scene and Dr. Hamm prepared the body for autopsy, Peter made himself and Zack ready for a manhunt.

He pulled a worn and loved T-shirt out of a zip lock bag and held it in front of Zack's nose. Bob had worn the shirt to bed the previous night, so it was well infused with his scent. An impromptu group of trackers stood by the back door of the bakery where Bob entered every morning.

"I didn't know Zack was trained in tracking," said Tom.

"Trailing, actually," said Peter. "Tracking works on the theory that dogs follow only the scent left by footprints. Their noses are forced toward the ground to keep them on the scent. Trailing allows the dogs to keep their noses up and follow scents in the air."

"And that's better?" asked Angus McLeod, oft borrowed deputy from nearby Deer Lodge County.

"Yes," said Peter. "Footprint scent trails can disappear on certain surfaces and are burnt off quickly on hot asphalt and concrete. Scents in the air are more stable."

Zack, wearing a trailing harness attached to a thirty-foot rolled bullhide lead, sniffed the shirt intently. Peter then let him sniff inside and outside the door and several feet into the alley. Zack ignored the Geary delivery truck parked outside and surrounded by crime scene tape, but suddenly stopped short and looked up at Peter, waiting for the order.

"Find," commanded Peter.

Peter and deputies Tom and Angus trotted to keep up with Zack who was hot on a trail. He led them through the alley toward Main Street. At Main Street, he took a sharp left turn and sniffed his way up the hill for several blocks, turning left again on

Lode Avenue. He led the men across the street and four houses up until he followed a concrete sidewalk to a bright blue front door fit into a sunshine yellow one-story bungalow with a neatly tended front yard.

"Wow!" said Angus. "That was quick. Do you think he's in there?"

"No," said Tom and Peter in unison.

"This is Bob's house," explained Peter.

Peter rang the doorbell. Linda Elliott opened the door, fresh faced and pretty in spite of her early morning.

"Hi Linda," said Peter. "Is Barb available?"

"She went to her bedroom a few minutes ago to take a nap but let me check. Dr. Hamm gave her a sedative. She's so worried about Bob."

"We need to ask her some questions," said Peter. "It's really important."

Before Linda could answer, Barb poked her head out the door, her short, box-blonde hair matted from sleep.

"That's okay, Linda," said Barb. "I didn't take anything yet. There's too much to think about to sleep."

She turned to Peter. "Did you find Bob?"

"We don't know where Bob is," he replied, "but I need to ask you some questions that may help us in our search."

"Okay."

"First," said Peter, "did Bob walk to work some-times?"

"He started walking a few weeks ago. His cholesterol is too high. Dr. Hamm told him if he didn't get the numbers down, he would have to start taking medication."

"That explains why Zack tracked him on the sidewalk," said Peter. "Do you know if he walked home from work last night? Could he have left his car in the lot and walked to work this morning?"

"No," said Barb. "I asked him to go to the grocery store and the hardware store on the way home. It would have been too hard to walk and carry things that far."

"Do you think he could be in the house some-where?" asked the ever-impatient Angus.

Peter gave him an exasperated look. Red headed and freckle-faced Angus, slightly built and wiry framed, was constantly in motion with nervous energy and the habit of butting into an interview process, skipping three questions ahead.

"Barb," said Peter, "we need to search the house and property just to verify that he isn't here some-where. Would you allow us to do that without a warrant?"

Barb hesitated, that same hesitation Peter noticed earlier when he asked her if there was any reason someone would want to hurt Bob.

"You can't possibly think Bob is hiding in the house somewhere," she said.

"Our tracking dog led us here and we need to search so we can put it in the police report. It's protocol," said Peter.

Tom and Angus nodded in agreement, although neither of them could remember that particular paragraph in any regulation manual.

Barb looked doubtfully at Zack wagging his tail and panting at Peter's feet.

"Oh, okay. But hurry, I need to rest. Leave the dog outside. I despise dogs."

Peter scratched Zack behind the ears and apologized as he secured his leash to the fence before trotting up the porch steps and into the house.

Linda offered to show the men through the house so Barb could rest, but Barb insisted she do it herself. She led the group through the three bedrooms and two baths on the main floor. The Dahl children had long ago grown and moved away. One of the spare bedrooms, converted to a sewing room for Barb, was filled floor to ceiling with quilting fabrics and a large sewing machine, the closet converted to storage shelves for quilting supplies. Peter was somewhat surprised considering the animosity between Margaret Franks of the quilt shop and the Dahls.

Barb, as if reading his mind, said, "I belong to a quilting group over at Nimrod."

The other extra bedroom, converted to an office for the bakery, overflowed with papers and books. In the middle of the mess sat a large antique oak desk.

"Do you mind if we look through the papers on Bob's desk?" asked Peter. "There may be a clue to his disappearance."

Barb wrung her hands. "I don't know. Bob doesn't like people in his stuff. He'll be mad if he finds out."

Peter sighed. "We don't have a clue how to find him, Barb. We don't even know which direction to start looking. Unless you're willing to help, there is no search for Bob. He may not be back."

"I'm too tired to think," said Barb. "Ask me again tomorrow."

Tomorrow may be too late, thought Peter, but he didn't want to push too hard.

When every room on the main floor was checked, including the living room, kitchen, and pantry, Peter asked about an attic and basement.

Barb showed the group a trap door in the ceiling of the hallway that led to an attic. Peter was about to send Tom out to the garage for a ladder when Barb pulled a ring that opened the door and released a retractable ladder. *Handy*, thought Peter. Angus, being the smallest, offered to go up the ladder and check out the space. He wasn't up there long when he poked his head through the opening.

"There's a lot of stuff up here to look through," he said. "I could use some help."

Tom followed Peter up the ladder. The attic space encompassed the entire area of the house and was crammed floor to ceiling with junk. The three of them explored every nook and opened every trunk, only to find the castoffs of ordinary life.

"Do you really think we're going to find Bob stuffed in a corner somewhere?" asked Tom.

"We need to be thorough," said Peter

Peter saw the skeptical looks from both Tom and Angus. They probably sensed that he wasn't actually looking for Bob. He was looking for a clue to what Barb was not telling him.

After sending Tom and Angus out to the detached garage, Peter briefly inspected the damp cellar filled with shelves of decades old forgotten jars of home-canned goods and wrinkled root vegetables past their prime. *Eventually, all that hard work will end up in a garbage bin*, thought Peter. Not seeing a disruption in the dirt floor to indicate a buried body or treasure, he climbed back up the rickety laddered steps to the main floor. He thanked Barb for her patience and assured her he would let her know as soon as he had any information on the whereabouts of Bob.

"Did you see anything interesting?" asked Peter when he and the deputies had reconvened on the sidewalk.

"Nothing much," said Angus. "I don't think that old shed has been used as a garage in a long time."

"More of a home for feral cats," said Tom, wrinkling his nose in disgust. "What do we do now?"

Peter untied Zack's leash and turned in the direction of the bakery. "We go back to the bakery and see if Zack can find another scent trail."

In the alley next to the rear door of the bakery, Peter allowed Zack the length of his leash to explore for another scent. Twenty minutes later, after Zack sniffed the alley on both sides from one end to the other, Peter had to acknowledge defeat.

"We can only make guesses at this point," he said to the other men. "He must have left in a car, either by choice or force."

5

Peter sent Tom and Angus to canvas the neighborhood for witnesses and drove back to his office to think. Bob was missing, Barb was hiding something, Sam Geary was dead. . . and Sam Geary was being threatened. Was Bob threatening Sam? Or were the calls and letters coming from Winston Hayes? Deep in thought, he didn't notice the commotion in the outer office until he was startled by a ringing phone. The blinking light told him it was from Travis's internal line.

"Hey, Trav. What's up?"

"Peter . . . you're not going to believe this."

"Try me."

"We have another body."

Peter swung his feet off his desk and sat up straight, suddenly very awake.

"What?! Who?"

"David Howard. Holly found him. She's here in the front office."

"Did she call it in?"

"No. I think she's in shock or something. She's pretty rattled. She came here first."

"Call Tom and Angus and tell them to go to David's house. They can finish the bakery neighborhood later."

Peter stood and walked into the outer office. Holly Noelle sat at Travis's desk, pale and shaking uncontrollably, her tightly wound caramel curls bouncing with each tremor, the blended green and brown of her almond eyes swimming in tears. Peter turned and walked back into his office. From out of a storage cabinet, he pulled the blanket he kept for those times when he had to stay overnight, and wrapped it around her shoulders.

"Get her some hot tea, Travis," said Peter.

While Travis boiled tea in the microwave, Peter pulled up a chair next to Holly, took her hand, and assured her everything would be okay.

Travis came back and handed Holly a cup of steaming Earl Grey. After several sips, she stopped shaking and was calm enough to answer questions.

"Tell me what happened," said Peter

"He's in his house," sobbed Holly.

She started to cry. Peter wrapped his arms around her and rocked her gently. He signaled Travis to send Tom and Angus to David's house.

When the sobs waned, Peter reheated Holly's tea, made a fresh one for himself, and led her into the more comfortable chair and privacy of his office.

"Okay," said Peter, "start at the beginning."

Holly took a deep breath.

"Uncle Dave didn't show up for the tour today. He didn't even call. I thought maybe he had his days mixed up. He only comes a couple days a week," she explained. "The bus needed to get going so I rode along and did the lecture."

Holly put her head in her hands. Her body shook with quiet sobs before she composed herself.

"Take your time," said Peter. "I know this is a terrible shock."

"I just can't get the image out of my mind. Just hanging there. His face all blue."

"I'll get more tea."

Holly let out a small laugh mixed with a sob.

"Oh, Peter. Time and tea heal all wounds. I haven't even taken a drink out of the last cup."

Peter smiled sheepishly. This time he plugged in the electric tea kettle he kept behind his desk.

"So, you went on the mine bus," he prompted.

"Yeah. I didn't really think of Uncle Dave all morning. I was busy with the group and the lecture . . . lots of younger kids today so that's always a handful. On the ride back, when things were calmer, I started worrying that he was too sick to call. He lives by himself and he's almost eighty."

Holly started to cry again.

"I should have checked on him in the morning. It wouldn't have mattered if the bus was late."

"It may not have mattered at all, Holly," said Peter. "He may have already been dead. We won't know anything until an investigation is done, including an autopsy."

"Still."

"You can't blame yourself. So, when the bus got back, then what?" asked Peter.

"I got everyone set up and sorting their buckets. One of the regulars was there, a guy from Missoula. Matthew. I said if he wouldn't mind watching out for everyone for a while, I would give him a refund for the day. He's helped me out in the past, even done some of the lectures, so he was good with it. I left and went to Uncle Dave's house. I have a key. When he didn't answer the door, I let myself in."

"The door was locked?"

"Yeah. He started locking his door night and day these last few years with so many outsiders in town and him on Main Street."

David Howard lived in a grand Victorian mansion on a hill on the east end of Main Street. In his family for generations, it was one of the most well-preserved houses in town. Red brick and white trim, with multiple porches, balconies, and towers, it stood on a well-landscaped lot that encompassed an entire city block. The mansion was often mistaken for a museum within a city park. Although surrounded by an ornate wrought iron fence, bolder tourists would open the gate and wander the grounds uninvited.

"About what time was this?" asked Peter.

"Around three or so."

"Where did you find him?"

Holly swallowed, holding back tears. "The staircase. The spiral one in the foyer. He was hanging over the edge with a rope around his neck."

"And then what did you do?"

"I wasn't thinking right. I ran out the door, got in my car, and drove here."

Peter's phone rang.

"Hey, Peter," said Tom. "We have the house and grounds taped off and secured, but a television crew from KRUD out of Missoula is already here. Someone called them and told them we have two murders . . . and Mavis is trying to push her way inside."

Mavis Vallee, the editor-in-chief and sole reporter of the local weekly, *The Anderson Chronicle*, had an office assistant and several freelance columnists, but insisted on covering anything considered breaking news herself, more out of a need for attention than a desire to report the news. Rarely seen wearing anything less than a well-cut pantsuit, towering high heels, and perfectly coifed platinum hair, Mavis was ever ready for a coveted television appearance.

"How on earth did the news people hear about this so fast?"

Holly managed a sheepish grin. "I'm sorry, Peter. I saw Mavis on the way into the courthouse. She asked me why I was so upset. I told her about Uncle Dave."

"I'll be right there," said Peter to Tom. "Don't let anyone in, especially Mavis, and 'no comment' to everyone."

"We'll do what we can. They're climbing over the back fence and looking through the windows."

"Send Angus out," said Peter. "Arrest anyone on the grounds and charge them with trespassing."

He disconnected and looked at Holly with concern. She was obviously still distressed.

"Go ahead," she said, irritated at being abandoned. "I'm fine. You have work to do, and I need to go back to The Sapphire Pit and take care of things."

Peter walked Holly out and drove to the Howard mansion, once again using his police lights to get through the crowd. To his dismay, the local food truck, moved from its usual spot on an empty lot by the brewery, was selling hamburgers and hotdogs to spectators. Girl Scouts hawked a variety of cookies from a brightly draped folding table. Mavis most likely sent messages out on social media to ensure a large crowd. Locals and tourists alike were using the death of David Howard as an entertainment event.

Like a flock of vultures, thought Peter as he shut off his engine and rolled down the Explorer windows.

"Stay, Zack!" he commanded as he closed the truck door and turned toward the mansion.

Peter pushed his way through a line of aggressive newspaper cameras and reporters. Mavis, being local and too familiar, grabbed his arm.

"Later, Mavis," he said, pushing her off. "I don't have any information yet."

He found Angus at the front steps with two nervous-looking young men, cameras and reporter's badges around their necks, sitting on the steps in handcuffs.

"I found them crawling through the back hedge," said Angus. "What do you want me to do with them?"

"Take down their names and the name of their employer. Write up an official warning, give them a copy and send a copy to their employer."

Both men howled in protest.

"Quiet, or we'll make it an official charge of trespassing," said Peter, reducing both men to silent glares.

Peter continued up the stairs and into the house. For the second time that day, he was met with a gruesome vision that would not soon leave his memory. Swaying under the balcony of the grand staircase was the corpse of David Howard. His face, as Holly had described, blue with death.

Tom sat on the stairs, face in hands. He didn't look up as Peter walked in.

"Tom!" barked Peter.

Tom jerked awake and almost tumbled down the stairs.

"Sorry, Pete. It's been a long day," he said looking up at the swinging corpse. "And stressful."

"Have you processed the crime scene?" asked Peter.

"I took a lot of pictures from every angle and dusted for fingerprints. Should we call Helen? She's really the expert at processing crime scenes."

"I'll check and see if she's done with the bakery."

He turned suddenly and ran back out the front door.

"Angus," said Peter. "Get casts of those reporter's shoes before they leave. We'll have to compare them to any other shoe prints we find to eliminate them as suspects."

Peter tapped Helen's number into his phone as he walked back into the mansion. Helen answered before the first ring.

"Peter! I heard there's another body. David Howard. How horrible! Do you want me to come over and process?"

"How are things at the bakery?" asked Peter.

"I've done all I can there. The ambulance crew came and collected the body. They transported it to the morgue. Dr. Hamm followed them out so I'm guessing he's doing the autopsy."

"Where are you?"

"I came home to clean up. Even with all that protective gear, I could still smell blood and death on me."

Peter nodded in understanding.

"Sure, Helen. I get it," he said. "Are you up to doing another scene? Tom got pictures and dusted for prints. He would feel more comfortable if you gave it a quick look over in case he missed anything."

"On my way."

Peter told Angus to wait for Helen and keep the gawkers off the grounds.

"Go home and take a nap," he said to Tom. "When you're awake, start a canvas of the neighborhood. Find out if anyone saw anything."

On his way to his vehicle, Peter stopped at the food truck and bought a bacon cheeseburger and fries for himself and four more for Zack, Angus, Travis, and Helen. He learned long ago to grab food when he could and with two bodies and a missing person, it was unlikely he or his crew would have a dinner break that day. Peter brought burgers into the house for Helen and Angus, and drove back to the courthouse, managing to keep drooling Zack out of the food bag until they were back in the sheriff's office. He handed a grateful Travis his food and then a burger to Zack who ate it in several gulps. Zack noisily lapped water from his bowl, curled up on his bed, and fell into a snoring sleep. Peter spread his lunch out on the paper sack on his desk, sat and chewed, and thought.

"Travis," he called out his open door. "Would you call over to the doctor's office and find out how the autopsy is going on Sam Geary? And let them know we need another one on David Howard ASAP."

"Sure, Boss," said Travis as he swallowed a bite of burger. Picking up the telephone, he punched the speed dial button for Dr. Hamm.

Peter sighed. The two people he really wanted to talk to were already involved with the cases. The first, Dr. Hamm, wouldn't have answers until both autopsies were complete. The second was Linda Elliott. Linda was Peter's second biggest secret as sheriff. As the wife of the pastor of the First Baptist Church and the head of the Christian Women's

Society, Linda not only knew everyone in town, she also knew everything about everyone in town, including intimate details and deep dark secrets. Peter knew Linda's deep dark secret. Linda, who had spent her youth as an avid reader, had become a successful author of murder mysteries as an adult. She published under a nom de plume and refused invitations to public book signings, keeping her real identity completely secret from her fans. When Linda wasn't attending to church functions, she was in her study in the parsonage typing away at her next novel.

Linda was also a very good detective, and Peter's confidant and advisor when he was analyzing a situation.

Peter got up and quietly closed his office door. He tapped in Linda's cell number.

"Hello," said Linda

"Are you still at Barb's?" asked Peter.

"Yes. She's resting peacefully."

"I could use some insight on this case."

"Several neighbor ladies are here for support so I can leave. Meet me at the parsonage."

"Congregant in need," she said to the other ladies as she headed out the door.

Peter waited a suitable amount of time for Linda to make her way home and then drove to the outskirts of town where the new Baptist church and parsonage were located. Paul, Peter's older brother and pastor of the church, answered the door.

"Hi, Pete. Come on in," said Paul, moving aside to let Peter and Zack pass through. "Linda said you were on your way over."

Paul, two years older than Peter but slighter in build, with darker hair and a scholarly air, was the only other person who knew of Linda's unofficial position as sheriff's consultant. Although Paul had no aptitude for investigation, he sat in on the brainstorming sessions and occasionally popped out with an idea that neither Peter nor Linda had considered.

"So," said Linda after they were settled around the kitchen table with tea for Peter and coffee for Linda and Paul. Fresh homemade ginger cookies were piled on a plate on the table. Zack sat underneath waiting for crumbs. "Fill us in on the details. I got some from Barb, but it was pretty garbled."

"Did you feel like she was hiding something?" asked Peter.

"Hmmmm. She's afraid of something," replied Linda. "I sat with her as she was dosing off. She mumbled something about Bob and then said, 'He should have gone to Peter.' Then she fell asleep."

Peter recounted both crime scenes and the conversation with Seth Geary. The three of them contemplated possibilities while they munched cookies.

Paul, whose greatest contribution to investigation lay in his organized mind, said, "Let's start at the beginning. Sam Geary. Who would want to murder him and why?"

"There's his son Seth," said Linda.

Surprised, Peter asked, "Seth? Why Seth? I never thought of him."

"He's the only one in the family who knew about the threatening letters and phone calls, and his prints were all over the letters."

"But he's the one who told Peter about them," countered Paul.

"Sure, but he had to have known, at least, the phone calls would be found in an investigation. He could be pointing suspicion toward that Winston Hayes guy. We only have his word about the fencing issue. Maybe he made the whole story up."

"And then there's Winston Hayes," said Peter. "If he's the one putting the letters in Sam's delivery truck, he's capable of following Sam into the bakery and knocking him over the head."

"Bob had issues with Sam, too," said Linda. "Maybe they got in an argument in the bakery about Bob's debt, Bob pushed him in the mixer, got scared, and made a run for it."

"How did he leave, though? His car is still in the parking lot?" said Peter.

"An accomplice?" asked Paul.

"That doesn't feel right," said Linda. "Something else was going on with Bob and I don't think it involved Sam Geary."

"Sam could have been in the wrong place at the wrong time," said Paul.

"If Bob was the target, wouldn't the murderer know he had the wrong person? Bob and Sam look nothing alike, even in the dark," said Linda.

"Any other ideas on those two?" asked Paul.

"Nope."

"Nope."

"What about David Howard?" asked Paul. "Was it a suicide or murder?"

"No idea," said Peter. "We'll have to wait for the autopsy on that one."

"I can't imagine anyone wanting to murder him. Everyone loved David," mused Linda. "He was the town patriarch."

"I certainly never saw him depressed or even sad," said Paul. "Suicide doesn't make sense either."

Peter wiped the crumbs off his shirt, and said to Linda, "Do you think you could convince Barb to let us look in Bob's office for clues?"

"I think so. It seems like she wants to confide in me, but I need to get her alone and clear-headed. I'll call and ask if she wants me to stay overnight."

Linda searched Barb's number on her cell phone and tapped the phone icon. When Barb answered,

Linda covered all the pleasantries and then offered to stay the night if Barb needed company.

"Sure, sure," Linda spoke into the phone. "I'll pack a bag and be over after dinner. Okay. No problem. Bye."

"All set. She sounded relieved not to be alone tonight."

"Great!" said Peter. "Thanks."

After Linda left the room to do her packing, Paul studied his brother's face. "How are you handling all of this?" he asked.

Peter shrugged. "As usual. I focus on the present."

Every law enforcement officer has those cases. The ones that hit them in the gut, and the heart, and mess with their heads. For Peter, murder triggered memories. Memories of the weekend Peter and his older brother Paul were left with neighbors while their parents celebrated their fifteenth wedding anniversary in Missoula. Memories of his father's smiling face and the warmth of his strong arms as he hugged Peter good-bye. Memories of his mother's perfume and the gentle kiss she left on his forehead. Memories of the Stone County sheriff standing on the doorstep of the neighbor's house, breaking the news of his parents' murder. That day forever changed the boys.

Reflective, ten-year-old Paul questioned why. What would cause someone to take another person's life. He studied the people around him and, even at his young age, he sensed a hurting humanity. He realized that hurting people hurt people. If he could help the hurting, he could stop the hurt. His contemplations led him to the church and the church led him to ministry.

Eight-year-old Peter felt anger and the need for justice. A move from their home in Princeton to nearby Anderson, and frail grandparents ill-equipped to raise young boys only increased his anger. Not only had he lost his parents, but now his home and friends. The same Stone County sheriff who brought the news that broke his heart stayed in his life and healed him. The sheriff, a father of two young boys himself, took Peter and Paul under his wing and into his family. He taught them to fish and hunt and camp and dig for sapphires. He taught them about honesty and the value of hard work. He taught Peter how to be a good sheriff. He taught Peter about justice.

Peter said his thanks and goodbyes and let himself out. He sat in his Explorer outside the parsonage, head in hands, massaging his scalp, burying his bad memories. Rather than risk going back to the office and getting pulled into more work, he called Travis for an update.

"Dr. Hamm finished the autopsy on Sam," said Travis. "He had to see patients this afternoon but said he would do the autopsy on David tomorrow morning and, barring any emergencies, give you the results of both tomorrow night. He was kind of cranky."

"We're all a little cranky today. Anything else pressing I need to deal with?"

"Nothing that can't wait," replied Travis. "Can I go home now?"

"Yes. Let's pray for a quiet night."

6

Angus, tom, and Travis were already eating donuts and sipping coffee in the outer office when Peter drug himself into work the next morning. He was once again reminded how much he depended on his two 'unofficial' deputies.

"Where'd you get the donuts?" asked Peter.

"Grocery store," said Tom, holding up a box of Little Debbies. "With the bakery out of commission we might have to start making them in-store."

Tom owned the local grocery store but managed it so well with the help of his wife and grown children, that he rarely needed to be there.

"Jake sent the paperwork over for me to stay here as long as I'm needed," said Angus between chews.

"You just need to sign and send it back . . . if you want me to stick around," he added.

"Thanks, Angus, I'll get it back to him this morning," said Peter, hiding his misgivings.

Jake McLeod, the sheriff in Rumsey where Angus was officially employed, was also Angus's uncle. Angus was well-qualified and capable, but his over-eager personality grated on Jake. Plus, there were occasional accusations of nepotism, which put scuff marks on Jake's political shine.

Peter needed the help in Stone County, but he dreaded the day Angus's tendency to jump into situations without thought would put himself or others in danger.

Peter filled his cup with water from the tap. The courthouse, like many buildings in town, was built next to a natural spring with a flow rate high enough to keep a cistern full and supply all the water needs of the building. Fresh spring water made for exceptional tea and coffee. Peter added two tea bags to his cup and nuked it for three minutes. Earl Grey, hot and strong, was his remedy for a groggy morning.

"Fill me in," he said to Travis, settling in for the morning update.

"One break-in, two lost dogs, Mavis wanting a statement, and a call from Margaret asking if we can shut the bakery down now. Does the woman have no soul?"

"Ignore Margaret and Mavis," said Peter. "Where was the break-in?"

"Barb Dahl's house. A neighbor saw a light on in the office when everyone should have been asleep."

"I'll take care of that one," said Peter, taking a sip of his tea. "Linda stayed with Barb last night. They were probably in the office sorting papers."

"I told the owner of the lost dogs to check animal control and then get back to us."

"Whose dogs?" asked Tom.

"Hobo Joe."

"Aaahhhh."

Hobo Joe, a rancid man of indiscernible age, lived in one of the few shacks in town that hadn't been demolished, mainly because he was living in it and had a clear title. Joe owned two mangy mutts to whom he was devoted. They were picked up several times a week, begging for food at various local restaurants. Most days, depending on who was on duty, animal control would drop them off at Hobo Joe's shack and save themselves the trouble of paperwork.

Thankful not to have any minor annoyances to deal with, Peter moved on to the major cases.

"Has Dr. Hamm called yet about the autopsies?" he asked Travis.

"Not to the main phone. He may have left a message on your office line. There have been a few calls in there."

"Did you guys hear anything interesting when you were canvassing the neighbors?" Peter asked Angus and Tom.

Tom pulled out his notebook and sighed. "Mrs. Brady, across the alley from the Howard place, swears she saw a white van with no license plates driven by Arabs go through the alley at four a.m. yesterday morning."

He looked over his glasses at Peter. "The woman can't see to find her back window and it was still dark. I checked. There is no way a person with good eyesight could have seen license plates or drivers over her back hedge."

"Okay. No need to follow up on that. Anything else?"

"Bert Harrison, on the other side, said he saw a dark vehicle, probably black, early that morning. We got the whole run down on his prostate. He gets up several times a night and doesn't always look at the clock so couldn't say for sure what time."

"Did he have a guess on what kind of vehicle?" asked Peter.

Tom looked at his notes. "He said, 'It was like a Suburban, but fancier.' "

"Obviously not a car buff."

"Nope."

"Anything else?" asked Peter.

"Not really. All the neighbors liked David. Great guy. Blah blah blah. Seemed happy. Lots of shock that he would hang himself."

"Okay, Bob Dahl, Sam Geary, and the bakery. Did anyone have a legitimate observation on that one?"

"Not really," said Tom. "It was too early in the morning for any of the other shop keepers to be out. Nobody was driving up Main Street at that time."

"Who called it in?" asked Peter.

"Couple guys on their way to Georgetown for dawn fishing. They saw Barb standing on the sidewalk screaming but chalked it up to a lunatic. They left their names and phone numbers when they called and said they didn't want to risk confronting her. I'm guessing the real reason is they didn't want to lose their place in line at the boat dock."

"Did you check them out?"

"Yeah. They're legitimate. Visiting from Wisconsin. Alibi checks out. They stopped for breakfast at the diner and were there right up to the time Barb was finding Sam's body."

"Dead ends," said Peter. "Oh, I almost forgot. I learned something interesting at the Gearys yesterday." He filled them in on the threatening letters and phone calls.

"There's a twist," said Angus. "Maybe Sam was the target after all."

"Possibly." Peter went into his office and unlocked the bottom desk drawer. He'd left the letters there in an evidence bag after the news of the second murder. After retrieving the letters, he walked back into the outer office.

"Gloves on everyone. Try not to smear the grease on the envelopes. We don't want to damage any fingerprints."

He opened the first letter and passed it around.

"Wow!" said Angus. "That's definitely a threat. Did Seth have any idea what this was all about?"

Peter recounted the story of the waterhole and the wrongly placed surveyor's stakes.

"State laws will side with the Gearys on that one," said Travis. "A border that has been agreed on over a hundred years is a legal border."

"I agree and so does Seth. He said Sam wasn't taking the threats seriously."

Peter opened the flap on the second envelope and read,

I'm watching you

Once again, he had a chill and sensed lurking evil. He passed the note around and reluctantly opened the third envelope. 'They get worse,' Seth had said.

I will destroy you and everything you cherish

And the fourth,

Your wife is pretty in blue....and so fragile

"This is over-the-top for a few feet of fence," said Tom. "Do you really think this Winston Hayes wrote these?"

"No idea, but I'm going out to his place today to have a chat with him. Another option is Bob Dahl. Bob owed Sam a lot of money and Sam was about to cut off his supply of dairy goods. Bob couldn't get them anywhere else on credit."

"Either one makes sense with the first letter. This Winston Hayes guy thinks the creek is his and Sam stole part of it. If Sam was going to cut off Bob's dairy supply, it would destroy his business. He would lose everything."

"That would explain why Bob disappeared. If he killed Sam, he would be on the run," said Angus.

"Exactly. Tom, can you handle traffic duty and routine calls today?"

"Sure, Boss. They certainly don't need me underfoot at the store."

"Angus, I'd like you to come along with me as backup. Winston Hayes may be a murderer."

"On it!" said Angus, standing and grabbing an extra donut from the box, prepared to follow Peter anywhere.

Peter stood and tossed his napkin into the trash and wondered, as he often did, if Angus would ever make the move and sign on full-time with Stone County. He whistled to Zack and prepared his mind for a possible dangerous confrontation.

"Do you know where we're going?" asked Angus when they were settled in the Explorer, Zack secure in his backseat kennel.

"Roughly. It's the ranch directly north of the Geary place. Run a driver's license check on Winston Hayes. Maybe we can GPS the address."

Several minutes later Angus groaned. "He has a Connecticut address."

"Well, that doesn't help. Seth did say he was from the East Coast. Do you know the name of an old guy with the last name of Murphy who died last spring?"

"Nope."

They drove Montana Highway 1, north from Anderson until the turnoff to Mary and Sam Geary's driveway.

"It should be the next place past here," said Peter.

A few miles up the road, a newly constructed ranch gate built of pine timbers set into stone pillars guarded an overgrown pasture gate. Hanging from the horizontal overhead beam was a sign bearing the brand 'W/H'.

"WH for Winston Hayes," said Angus. "I think we're here."

Peter turned the Explorer into the gate and onto a rutted dirt road. "Fancy entrance leading to a dirt track. I wonder what that's all about," he said.

They maneuvered the bumpy lane at minimal speeds and maximum jostling. A particularly deep hole had Angus banging his head against the window.

"Ouch! This better be worth it."

He rubbed his head and hit the button on the side of the door to let the window down. Peter did the same although it was hard to enjoy the country pleasures of birdsong and the scent of heat-warmed wildflowers when you were concentrating on staying on track.

The road wound its way past a stand of Aspen trees and gradually up a hillside where it leveled out onto a wide plateau. Construction was underway on what would be a massive timber and stone-pillared house matching the ranch entrance.

Peter stopped a suitable distance away as to not hinder construction and parked. He told Zack to stay while he and Angus stepped out of the Explorer. A cowboy in worn blue jeans, faded flannel shirt, and worse for wear cream colored straw cowboy hat, eased himself off the hood of a battered ranch truck and strode toward them.

"Is there a problem, Sheriff?"

"I'm looking for a Winston Hayes."

The cowboy stiffened. "You won't find him here."

"Is this his place?"

"Yeah, but like I said, he's not here."

"Do you know where I could find him?"

"Somewhere in Connecticut."

"Who would you be?"

"Clay Pidgen. I'm the ranch foreman here. Can I ask what this is about?"

"Has Mr. Hayes been here recently?"

"Mr. Hayes has been here a total of once since he bought the place. I've worked here for the Murphy family for thirty-four years. I guess I should be grateful Mr. Hayes decided to keep me on."

"Is he planning on moving here when the house is finished?"

"I doubt it. He's not much interested in actually running the ranch. I get the feeling he has money to burn and likes the idea of owning a ranch in Montana."

"Do you know anything about a border dispute between Mr. Hayes and Sam Geary?"

Clay tilted his head to the south and gestured toward a decent-sized creek meandering through the lower meadow. A curve of the creek flowed under a neighboring fence, but eventually made its way back.

"Is that the waterhole in question?" asked Peter.

"That's it. When he came here, Mr. Hayes had a copy of the official plat map for the ranch. He insisted on being driven around the entire property, which is impossible. There isn't a road. When he realized he'd have to either walk or get on a horse, he backed down, but started picking apart the places he could see. His map showed the entire creek on his property. He demanded the fence be moved. I told him he had no legal right to that property after all these years. I thought he was going to fire me."

"Not a nice guy?" asked Angus.

"No. A real jerk, but at my age, I don't want to think about finding a new job."

"Do you think he's the kind of guy who would harass and threaten Sam Geary about that property?"

"Oh, yeah. He's the kind of guy who pulls the wings off flies just to see them suffer."

"But he hasn't been in the area?"

"Not that I know of. He came that once and stayed a couple days in the old ranch house. It's a mile or so down the road, not fancy enough for him. I live there now and he's having this place built."

"I didn't notice any cows in the pasture," said Peter.

"All sold off when old man Murphy died. I just keep the hay mowed and my eye on the construction company, but the pay is good."

"Do you have contact information for Mr. Hayes?"

"Sure. Hold on."

Clay walked back to the truck and rummaged through the glove box. He came back holding a dirt-smudged business card.

"He left me a stack of these."

"Thanks," said Peter. "You'll let me know if there are any new developments on that land issue?"

"Will do."

Peter and Angus got into the Explorer.

"What do you think?" asked Angus.

"Winston Hayes could have made the threatening calls from Connecticut, but the letters were put directly in Sam's truck. It would have to be someone local or at least within driving range."

"That's what I was thinking, but who?"

"No idea. When we get back, I want you to call the closest airports and police stations connected to the address on this card. See if you can find out if Winston Hayes has flown into Montana recently. Do you have a pair of nitrile gloves handy?"

Angus pulled a pair out of his front shirt pocket.

"Always."

"Put them on."

Peter handed Angus the business card, still pinched between his finger and thumb.

"The top left corner will have my prints. When we get back, cover the phones for Travis so he can get this along with those letters and envelopes set up in the fuming chamber."

"Fuming chamber?"

"Yeah. For lifting fingerprints."

"We have one of those?" said Angus, impressed.

Peter laughed. "We have a whole forensics room. Have Travis give you a tour."

Back at the courthouse, Peter and Angus filled Travis in on Winston Hayes and his hired man, Clay Pidgen.

"Forward the phones upstairs, Travis. You can give Angus a tour of the forensics room and show him how to use the equipment. When you're done, Angus, don't forget to make those phone calls to Connecticut."

"Sure, Boss."

Travis motioned Angus to follow him to the back corner of the room. Next to an old antique filing cabinet was an equally old door. Behind the door, a dark narrow stairway led to a surprisingly bright room, the outer wall filled with windows and the remaining space with work counters and modern forensics equipment, including a top-of-the-line fuming chamber.

"Wow! You must have some budget."

"We have a generous benefactor who loves crime-scene investigation shows."

"Cool!"

Meanwhile, Peter sat at his desk and, as was his habit when thinking, combed his fingers through his hair until it stood upright. He had dealt with many deaths through the years, but they were always straightforward. Death by natural causes, easily-determined murders, or suicide by various methods, all required minimal investigation to prove the cause. Whatever happened with Bob Dahl, Sam Geary, and David Howard had him baffled with no solid leads to point him in the right direction. He glanced down and noticed the message light on his desk phone blinking. He pushed the button and heard Holly's voice.

"Hi Peter. Just checking in."

He could hear her struggling, trying not to cry.

"I know you . . . have a lot on your plate now . . . but I'm . . . I'm not in a good place. I need to talk. If you get some time . . . please call me."

Peter took a deep breath and let it out slowly. Holly. He didn't know how he felt about Holly. She broke up with him years ago in a fit of rage yet called him whenever she needed a shoulder for crying, or a handyman for her century-old cottage or a ride when her car broke down. And he always came.

The ringing of the phone roused Peter out of his musings.

"Sheriff's office."

"Hey, Peter. This is Dr. Hamm."

Peter moved his feet off his desk and sat up straight. "What did you find?"

"Sam Geary was struck on the back of the head with a heavy object . . . looks suspiciously like an aluminum baseball bat. The blow didn't kill him. The person who struck the blow either wasn't very strong or didn't put much effort into it. Sam was still alive when he went into the mixer. I'm guessing he woke up in time for the mechanical force of the mixer to sever his right leg at the hip. Cause of death was exsanguination through the femoral artery."

"Plain English please, Doc."

"He bled to death when the mixer tore his leg off and ripped the artery in half . . . he was probably conscious when it happened. Not a pleasant death."

Peter groaned.

"Barb Dahl says Bob went in at four and she was there by five-fifteen so we can probably narrow it down to that for time of death."

"Sounds about right. I'll add that to the report."

"Okay, thanks. Anything on David Howard yet?"

"On my way to the morgue now. It will take me a few hours. I'll let you know."

"Thanks, Doc."

Peter rang off, put on his hat, and whistled for Zack. Comforting Holly in person was always better than over the phone.

7

"So, you don't think it was suicide?" asked Peter.

"Evidence points at murder," said Dr. Hamm. "It wasn't what you would think of as a typical hanging, there was no hangman's fracture."

"What's that?"

"When a body is dropped suddenly from a height, the weight of the body causes the odontoid process, a small bone on the second vertebrae, to snap off. The broken piece is forced forward severing the spinal cord. Death is quick and painless. Hanging, as gruesome as it seems, is actually a very humane form of execution when done correctly."

"Uh, okay. If you say so. What's different about this hanging?"

"David's neck wasn't broken, but that isn't definitive for a complete hanging. If the height of the drop and the weight of the body aren't well calculated, death will result from strangulation. Proper hanging is an art form. In this case, ligature marks on the neck indicate the body was slowly pulled up and tied off. There are several rows of rope marks before the final position that resulted in strangulation. He couldn't have done that himself."

"You seem to know a lot about hanging," reflected Peter, wondering if he should put the doctor on his suspect list.

"A professor in medical school was a hanging enthusiast. We actually had to write a term paper on hanging methods and differentiating murder and suicide."

Coming in handy now, thought Peter. "Anything else?"

"Lots. The rope was tied in the occipital position . . . with the knot at the back of the neck. Statistically, suicides rarely have the knot in that position. They're generally at the front of the neck, more easily accessed by the victim, but that's speculation."

"Any more solid facts?" prompted Peter. The doctor had a tendency to start rambling when he was on a favorite medical subject.

"The bluish tinge in his face and fingernails, and hemorrhages in his eyes point to strangulation rather than hanging," said Dr. Hamm "But here's the interesting stuff. He had vomit down the front of his shirt. That could have happened before or after the lynching but isn't a sign of strangulation. Also, there are no scratch marks or other signs that he fought the hanging. Nothing is definitive, but I have a hunch he was sedated or poisoned before he was strung up. I sent his stomach contents into the forensic lab in Missoula."

"How long will that take?"

"I have a good friend there. He's handling it personally. He said sometime tomorrow unless someone more powerful with a bigger problem cuts the line."

"Approximate time of death?"

"He was still in full rigor mortis. Livor mortis was complete. A guesstimate would be between twelve and twenty-four hours before his body was found."

"About what we thought. Thanks, Doc. Keep me posted."

Peter picked up his phone and punched Travis's internal line.

"Yeah, Boss?"

"Do you know where Helen is?"

"Out here typing reports. Should I send her in?"

"Yes, please. Thanks."

Helen came in looking cranky and disheveled.

"If they were going to murder someone, couldn't they have picked a place nobody cared about? Like the health food store."

"Missing your afternoon donut and coffee?" asked Peter.

"Yes. I'm exhausted. Two crime scenes yesterday and then night-shift traffic duty."

"The grocery store has donuts."

She looked at him with a mix of disbelief and disgust. "Yeah, prepackaged chemical cakes. I'm a donut connoisseur with refined tastes," she added with an affected accent.

"Biscotti and a cup of Earl Grey?"

"Ugggh. Okay. Better than nothing. Thanks"

Peter poured Helen a cup of hot water and dropped in a tea bag. He set a plastic tub of chocolate-covered almond biscotti on his desk.

"Knock yourself out."

When she had settled in with her snack, he asked, "Did you find anything significant at either place?"

"Starting with the bakery? Nothing. No sign of forced entry. It looked like Bob was set up to start a routine day, flour and stuff set out on the counter. The only footprints were ours. Whoever shoved Sam in that mixer was gone before the blood started spraying. We don't have fingerprints on Bob, but compared to prints we took from their house, the only prints in the back room are from Bob and Barb.

There are a few from Sam, but only where you would expect them. There are prints on the front till and back of the display cases that we assume belong to Sally. Travis left a message for her to come in and get printed so we can confirm that. There are tons of prints on the front of the display cases, drink coolers, tables, and chairs. We would have to track down and print every customer to sort through those. I personally don't think it's worth the effort."

"Agreed. No footprints out the back door?"

"Gravel lot and dry. Nothing to leave footprints in. Nobody in town has security cameras. Welcome to Mayberry."

"Anything else interesting?"

Helen smiled a sly smile and set an evidence bag containing an envelope onto Peter's desk.

"Another threat letter?" he asked.

"Yep. I found it on the front seat of Sam's delivery truck. It was already opened, so Sam had it before he went into the bakery."

Peter opened his bottom drawer and pulled a pair of nitrile gloves out of a box. He opened the evidence bag, removed the envelope, and the most recent letter written like the others on a piece of composition paper.

Your time is almost up.

"His time is up," mused Peter.

"There's no telling how long that letter was in the truck," said Helen. "Sam wasn't a slob, but there were breakfast-sandwich wrappers and Styrofoam coffee cups from several days on the floor. He didn't clean it out every day."

Peter slipped the letter and envelope back into the evidence bag and sighed. "Okay, next mystery. Did you find anything at David's house? A suicide note?"

"Not that we found. Typical papers on his desk . . . bills, personal correspondence, bank statements." She lifted a canvas satchel onto Peter's desk. "Here it is if you want to go through it."

"Thanks. Sign of a struggle or forced entry?"

"No, but there was a piece of pie on the kitchen table . . . a couple bites out of it and another on the fork. It looked like he was interrupted while he was eating and never came back."

"Hmmm. So maybe someone he knew came to visit. Does he have a doorbell or knocker?"

"Both. The knocker for show and the doorbell a concession to modern convenience."

"Fingerprints?"

"On the doorbell, but there are so many smudged together there's no way we would get a definite 'last visitor' print."

"Well, ask around. Find out if anyone will admit to visiting him Monday night. You did fingerprint the rest of the house?"

She gave him an 'I'm not stupid' look.

"The house is covered in fingerprints. I couldn't see any sign of someone trying to wipe things clean. We fingerprinted David and his cleaning woman, Susan Rice. Most of the prints are from them. Susan comes in on Mondays, so they were fresh. There were no hits in the national fingerprint database on the unknowns. Footprints by the window were all from the reporters Angus caught snooping. There are multiple footprints all around the grounds. They could be from reporters or tourists or nosy Nancys. Too hard to trace."

"Agreed. Let me know if you come up with anything else."

Peter stood and snagged the satchel of paperwork and evidence bag holding the newest threat letter and followed Helen out.

"Here, Travis. This is paperwork from David Howard's house, also another threat letter for Sam. Work your magic."

Travis's eyes lit up. He washed out of the public side of police work but excelled in investigation. Spending hours poring over telephone records and the like was his passion.

"Thanks, Boss!" said Travis. "By the way, you might want to take a look outside."

Peter heard a ruckus through the open window and leaned out to investigate. A television van from KRUD in Missoula was parked across the street and crewmen were unloading equipment. A crowd gathered on the lawn in front and around the courthouse steps and flowed into the street. Mavis Vallee and Anderson's Mayor Dwight Kalinski had a podium set up on the steps and were holding court. The mayor had control of the microphone.

"Once again, Sheriff Elliott is proving his incompetence," they heard the mayor announce. "We have two murders and a missing person, and he is hiding on the second floor of this very building, refusing to investigate."

Peter's blood boiled.

"Wow. What does he have against you?" asked Helen.

"I refuse to fix his endless parking tickets. Handicap spaces, loading zones, in front of fire hydrants. The street could be completely empty, and he would park in the only restricted spot."

"Still. That's pretty vicious for a few parking tickets."

"A lot of parking tickets," said Travis, who did the processing.

Mayor Kalinski was mayor only because the previous mayor and more popular candidate died of a heart attack on election night. The deceased incumbent won the race, but Dwight Kalinski was appointed by default. Mayor Kalinski led with greed, arrogance, and a 'me first' leadership philosophy.

Peter went into his office and lifted his Stetson off its hook. Press conferences required a Stetson.

"Stay, Zack."

He paced himself walking down the hall and stairway to the front doors of the courthouse, breathing deeply to dilute his anger. Confronting the likes of Mavis and the mayor always went better with a clear head.

Mavis had control of the microphone when Peter walked through the doors. "We have to ask ourselves 'Why do murderers feel comfortable walking our once-peaceful streets?'"

Her look of surprise and guilt when he put his large hand over hers and commandeered the microphone extinguished any remaining ire. *Will you ever learn, Mavis?*

Peter heard the clatter of shoes, grunts, and cursing as Mavis and the mayor jostled each other to get through the door.

He turned to the crowd. "Contrary to recent comments, our office is actively investigating both murders and the missing-person case. Our local physician, Dr. Hamm, has conducted autopsies. And our forensics expert, Helen Ferguson, has processed both crime scenes."

"Are the three incidents connected?" asked a reporter.

"I can't comment on current investigations, but I can assure you, our department is actively investigating all three incidents."

"Do you think your handling of these investigations will hurt your chances of re-election?"

"We'll let the voters think for themselves."

Ignoring further questions, Peter reached down and unplugged the microphone from the extension cord that was trailing from inside the courthouse.

Travis laughed when he saw Peter walk in with the microphone. "Another confiscation?"

"Yep."

Travis opened the bottom drawer of their antique oak filing cabinet and watched as Peter dropped the microphone on top of a growing pile.

"How many do you suppose we have?"

"Not enough as long as either one of those bozos have one in their possession."

8

PETER'S PHONE DINGED. Linda.

"Hi, Peter. I'm home from Barb's. If you get a chance, could you come over? I found something interesting in Bob's office."

"Was Barb okay with that?"

"Yeah. With her head clear of the sedatives, she was more worried about finding Bob than him being mad at us for invading his office. She let me bring this home."

"Did she open up about anything else?"

"A little. I'll tell you about it when you get here."

"Were you looking through things last night? A neighbor reported burglars at Barb's house because the office lights were on after what she considered bedtime."

"Wow! Talk about nosy neighbors. It was probably me. Promise I wasn't snooping without permission. I couldn't sleep so I was looking through the bookcase for something to read."

"What did you pick?"

"*Cooking With Plants That are Both Edible and Poisonous.*"

"Interesting choice."

"There wasn't much to choose from. Apparently, Barb doesn't read. I couldn't even find a steamy romance. Bob's only interest was . . . is baking."

Peter had a sudden epiphany. Dr. Hamm was suspicious that David had been poisoned. Helen said a half-eaten piece of pie was on the table.

"Peter?" said Linda "Are you there?"

"Oh, sorry, Linda. I just had a thought. I'll give you a call back in a while. I have to take care of something."

Peter punched in Helen's number. "Helen. The pie David was eating. Is it still there?"

"Yeah. Just like he left it. The rest of the pie is sitting on the kitchen counter."

"Is just the one piece out?"

"Two pieces are gone, including the one David was eating."

"Bag it and bring it in. I'll explain when you get here. Don't eat any!!!"

Peter tapped in Linda's number. "I'm on my way."

Linda opened the door, with a gleeful look, before Peter had a chance to knock.

"I think I have a clue," she whispered, looking both ways down the street.

She led Peter into her study. Several stacks of papers were laid out across the desk.

"You took these from Bob's office?" asked Peter.

"Yeah, Barb was good with it."

Peter examined the stacks. The first was bank statements going back several years. Balances started out extremely low, including numerous overdraft notices. Then there was a large deposit of $500,000. Peter moved on to the next stack. It was invoices for new equipment for the bakery, including the giant floor mixer. Bob remodeled the entire bakery so there were also bills from contractors and building supply companies. Invoice dates corresponded to the date of the large deposit.

"Have you looked through these?" asked Peter.

"Yeah."

"It looks like Bob got a loan to update the bakery. We knew about that. It happened after Margaret filed that first complaint. The health department said he needed to update equipment. It was a safety issue rather than cleanliness.”

“Maybe,” said Linda. “But I added up the invoices. The amount of money deposited is way over what he needed for the remodel and equipment.”

“Well . . . okay,” said Peter, contemplating a connection between the money and Bob’s disappearance. “But we don’t know where he got the money.”

Peter moved on to the next pile. “What’s this?” he asked.

“Plat maps of Anderson and Stone County. They show lot and property boundaries and names of the owners.”

“Have you studied these?”

“Yes,” said Linda, once again with that look of glee.

“And . . . what did you find?” prompted Peter.

“Did you know that Bob owns all the land along the east side of the highway next to Anderson?”

“Wow. Really?”

“For about five miles in each direction.”

“Maybe he got the money from selling land.”

“Guess who owns the same amount of land on the other side of the highway.”

“Not a clue.”

“David Howard.”

Peter looked at Linda with his mouth open, speechless.

"Seems like a clue to me," said Linda, laughing at his expression.

"It's definitely a connection."

"Look at the next pile." Linda nodded toward the desk.

Peter picked up the top sheaf of papers on the last stack. Large ornate print from a bygone era proclaimed 'Last Will and Testament of' in faded ink. On a line below was written, 'Charles William Anderson.'

"I'm assuming you also read through this?" asked Peter.

"It's the will of Charles Anderson. He owned most of the land in Stone County. Anderson was named after him. I went to the historic society this morning and looked it up. Apparently, the settlement began as a blacksmith's forge for the far side of the ranch. The ranch was so enormous they had cowboys who did nothing but ride back and forth to the main ranch for horseshoes and nails and stuff. The new forge kept them off the road and working the cows. Eventually, they put in a general store. Some of those guys went years without actually going back to the main ranch or talking to the boss. He always had a foreman covering for him."

"No kidding. So, Anderson started as a settlement for those cowboys."

"Started. Then gold and silver miners came, and the ranch sold supplies to them. And to neighboring homesteaders. It was a lucrative business. They opened a saloon and a hotel, too."

"So, lots of land and lots of money. How does this connect to David Howard and Bob Dahl?"

"They fit somewhere down the family tree. I'm not sure of the lineage."

Peter set down the will and picked up the paper underneath.

"What's this?"

"The covenants tied to the Andersons' land. Old Charlie made sure he was still in control all these generations later."

Peter's phone dinged.

"Hey, Peter," said an annoyed Helen. "Where are you? I've been waiting with this pie for half an hour."

"Sorry. I'm in the middle of something else. Package a few pieces up and send them to toxicology in Missoula. Freeze the rest. Don't eat any!!!" he reminded her. "I'll be there in a bit."

Helen inspected the smear of pie filling she had almost licked off her finger out of habit. Yikes, that was close.

Peter picked up the last stack of paperwork, the top sheet labeled 'Site Plans, Andersonville, BBR Architecture'.

"These are architectural drawings."

"They're plans for a huge resort to be built along the highway next to Anderson. Hotels, casinos, pools, even stables and riding paths winding around a man-made lake."

"This was all just sitting out on his desk?" Peter asked Linda.

"Well, that's the interesting thing," she said. "I was looking through his drawers for clues and the bottom drawer was locked. Barb didn't know where he hid the key, so I kept snooping around. Guess where I found it."

"Taped under the edge of the desktop," he said sarcastically.

"Bingo." She laughed. "Not very creative."

"Was there anything else in the drawer?"

"When I first opened it, I was kind of disappointed. It was just hanging file folders with business invoices, bills and stuff. Nothing interesting. Then I pulled it all forward and found a box with all these papers."

Glancing down at the piles of paperwork, Peter asked Linda, "Do you mind if I take this back to the office to read?" He didn't want her to feel like she was being ousted from the investigation.

"Sure," she said. "I've already read them all. But keep me in the loop, okay?"

"Oh, yeah." Peter headed toward the door. "You said Barb opened up about what was going on with Bob."

"She doesn't know much. Bob took care of all the business stuff and their personal finances."

"So, she wouldn't have known if he wasn't paying their bills?"

"He didn't even allow her to go into his office. That's why she was so touchy about it when you were there. She said he's been really stressed the last couple of years, but she thought it was because of the bakery remodel and dealing with all the contractors and learning the new equipment. Plus, business has tripled with the influx of tourists. They can hardly keep up with the baking and haven't been able to find reliable help."

"You don't think she's hiding anything?"

"I almost forgot. She said he's been getting a lot of strange calls lately . . . all hours of the day . . . late at night. He gets nervous and upset but won't tell her what's going on."

"And she didn't mention that. Why?"

"She thought it made Bob 'look bad.'"

While driving back to the courthouse, Peter contemplated the things people held back in an investigation and the reasons for doing so. Barb, ironically, held back a detail that could help save her husband's life in order to save his reputation.

He found Travis and Helen so engrossed in their work that they didn't hear him walk into the outer office.

"What are you two up to?" he asked.

"Hey, Peter," said Helen, not looking up from her work.

Travis kept typing on his computer.

"Well...," said Peter.

"Oh, sorry, Peter," said Travis. "I'm tracing the calls from David's phone bill. Helen is going through his bank statements, looking for irregularities."

"Good. Find anything interesting yet?"

"He had a lot of calls from Bob Dahl in the last few weeks."

"Were they friends?"

"Not that I know of. David was friends with everyone. Bob, not so much."

"Really? Why?"

"Bob's kind of a scoundrel. People don't trust him."

"And he's a horrible neighbor," said Helen, who lived several blocks down Lode Street from Bob and Barb. "He complains of noise when people mow their lawns in the middle of the day or kids who ride their bikes down the street. He thinks everyone should go to bed at two in the afternoon just because he does."

"He's always threatening to shoot neighbor dogs for chasing Barb's cats," said Travis. "She has dozens of feral cats living in that old garage out back. They mess in everyone's flower beds and chase birds from the feeders."

"Weird. He was always so happy and friendly in the bakery."

"Putting on an act for the customers," said Helen

"Did he have any beefs with David?" asked Peter.

"Not that I know of," replied Helen. "Hey, Peter, what's the deal with the pie?"

"Doc thinks David was poisoned. The pie sitting there half eaten makes sense. We sent his stomach contents to toxicology. If the same thing is in the pie, we've got our answer."

"I doubt it was the pie," said Helen.

"Why?" asked Peter.

"Because he got it from Holly."

Peter did a poor job of covering his surprise. "How do you know it was from Holly?"

"I found a card under the pie pan."

She walked over to her work bench, picked up an envelope, and handed it to Peter. He noticed her nitrile gloves and said, "Hold on while I put on gloves."

Hands covered, he took the envelope from Helen. The small cream-colored envelope, addressed to David in dainty and precise printed letters, told him immediately that it wasn't from Holly. Holly's handwriting was bold and ornate. Inside the envelope was a card imprinted with a bouquet of flowers and the words 'THANK YOU!' in large black letters on the front. Inside the card, in the same dainty printing as on the envelope, was written: 'Thank you for all your help at The Sapphire Pit and for handling that difficult situation today.'

"Unless she got someone else to write the card for her, this isn't from Holly. But whoever wrote it knew about the incident at The Sapphire Pit."

Travis looked at the clock. "She should be off the mountain by now. Do you want me to bring her in for questioning?"

Peter's stomach clenched. He and Holly had spent a companionable evening together the night before, tears intermixed with laughter as they shared stories of her Uncle David. He fingered the ring he carried in his pocket now and then, hoping someday she would take it back. An interrogation wouldn't go over well.

"We'd better," said Peter. "We can't exclude her as a suspect because we like her. Was there anything else with the pie that would tell us where it came from?"

"It looks homemade, not pre-frozen store bought," said Helen. "There wasn't a bakery box in the garbage and the pie tin is a generic throw away."

"Great," said Peter. "One more mystery with no clues. I'm guessing no fingerprints on the pie tin."

"Nope. Wiped clean."

"So, David ate poison, presumably from the pie, and then hung himself?" asked Travis.

"Dr. Hamm is sure the hanging was murder, not suicide."

"Someone sent him a poisoned pie and then strung him up for good measure?" asked Helen.

"Unless the pie and hanging are unrelated. At least one someone wanted him dead," said Travis. "But who would want to murder David. Everyone liked him."

"What about that psycho mom from The Sapphire Pit you were telling us about?" asked Helen. "She might be nuts enough to come back for revenge."

"All the way from Missoula to murder a guy over that spoiled brat kid of hers?" asked Peter.

Helen shrugged. "People have murdered for less."

"I guess we'd better check it out. Travis, when you call Holly, would you ask her to bring in the contact info on that family from The Sapphire Pit? She should have it. Everyone is supposed to fill out an information sheet when they sign up for the bus ride."

"Sure, Boss." Travis reached to pick up the telephone.

Peter walked into his office and brought out the long folding table he kept in the closet for occasions like this. He spread the paperwork from Bob's desk into neat piles along its length.

Hearing slow deep echoes of boots in the hall, Peter looked up in time to see a tall cowboy standing in the doorway. His clothes were neat and fit him well, but he was awkward in the wearing of them. His face, as well, was unaccustomed to shaving, judging by hints of irritation along the jawline. The eyes were troubled and red-rimmed, belying the smile and outstretched hand greeting Peter.

"John!" exclaimed Peter, ignoring the handshake and giving the old hermit a hug. He held him at arms-length. "Holly told you about David?"

"She called. It took me this long to find someone to mind the flock. I didn't know how long I would be away," he added softly.

Noticing a paleness in John's face and a slight tremor in his hands, Peter asked, "Have you had anything to eat, John?"

"Gosh," he said, looking slightly surprised at himself. "I've been so busy pulling these clothes out of mothballs and making arrangements for the apostles," as he called his sheep, "I didn't think about food."

"Hey, you guys," Peter said, grabbing John by the arm and motioning to Helen and Travis. "We all need a break. Dinner on the county."

Helen grinned, jumping up from her chair so fast it tipped over and clattered to the floor. Her face turned a bright crimson as she hurried to set it upright.

Travis laughed, but then frowned and nodded his head toward the phone. "Who's gonna to man the phones, Boss?"

"Transfer them to your cell. We'll all cross our fingers nothing important happens in the next couple hours."

The price for dinner would come out of Peter's own pocket, but he didn't want arguments, especially from John Anderson. He called Angus and Tom and told them to take a break and meet at The Grill, then called The Grill and told them to have a table ready for six. John, unaccustomed to civilization, would be more comfortable with the least amount of fuss.

John Anderson, brother to David Howard, and father to Holly, spent all but the coldest months of winter living in the mountains with nothing but his dogs and sheep for company. Before snow accumulated to the point of stranding John and his flock on the mountain, he and the pair of Great Pyrenees who stood guard over the flock year-round, made their way down to the safety and comfort of the ranch house and barns. Once shearing and lambing were complete in early spring, he would swamp out and restock his sheep wagon, and meander back to the mountains.

Angus was already seated when the group arrived. Tom came soon after, with Holly in tow.

"Look who I found on her way to the sheriff's office," he said.

Travis quickly pulled another chair next to the large round table and motioned to the waitress for an extra menu and glass of sweet spring water, fresh out of the tap in Anderson.

Holly cried, "Daddy!" when she saw John and gave him a giant hug. "When did you get here?"

"Just a bit ago. You were out with the bus." John gave her a concerned look. "Can't you take some time off while we're dealing with things here?"

"My friend Matthew is coming from Missoula tomorrow. He'll run things as long as I need him."

Peter felt a twinge of jealousy. He knew of Matthew, with the gem shop in Missoula, but didn't realize until now Holly considered Matthew a close friend. Trusting him to run her business indefinitely was significant.

John noticed Peter's reaction. He hoped Holly wasn't making a mistake. His eyes filled with tears. "Who would do this, Peaches?"

"I don't know, Daddy. Everyone loved Uncle Dave. Peter and the crew are doing everything they can."

With that, they gathered around the table and, no communication necessary, piled their menus in the middle unread. The Grill had 'world-famous' barbecue ribs that trumped the other options on the menu. Locals rarely ordered anything else.

When the waitress came by with plastic bibs and piles of napkins, Holly jumped up and helped her dad tie a bib around his neck, no doubt worried he would take his shirt off to save it from getting dirty. John had become somewhat eccentric in his shepherding years. With limited ability to wash clothes in the mountains short of scrubbing them on rocks in the creek, he had, reasonably, stopped wearing them, keeping a good set for 'going to town.' John spent his early years at seminary and then pastoring a church of his own, only giving up the pulpit with the devastating death of his wife, Holly's mother. He continued to preach, loudly proclaiming his message to a flock of sheep in the mountains rather than a flock of believers in church. Couple that with letting his hair and beard grow out long and gray rather than bother with the hassle of trims, the intelligent, well-educated man came across as a modern-day John the Baptist. Periodically, Peter received a complaint from a wandering hiker about a naked 'crazy' guy running around on the mountain. Peter would calmly explain that the hiker had been trespassing and he would let the charge go if they promised to use a GPS device in the future.

Waiting for the food to arrive, Peter studied the people gathered around the table, mostly coworkers. Tom was the only one who wasn't single. There were no last-minute scooting chairs around the table to make room for late arriving spouses, no children in highchairs and booster seats. Was it the job? Years ago, his entire future had been planned around a life and family with Holly. Now he went home to an empty house, a house Holly had picked out.

"Here you go, Sheriff." The arrival of platters of ribs and bowls of coleslaw interrupted Peter's musings.

"Where's your better half tonight?" he asked Tom, as he filled his plate.

"She was going to a Tupperware party or some such thing. I'm going to have to build an addition onto the kitchen to store all the Tupperware we have now."

"A girl can never have enough Tupperware," laughed Holly.

Good to know, thought Angus, always taking mental notes into Holly's psyche.

After a long enjoyable dinner, the group pushed back their plates and collectively declared they would call it a day and go home to bed.

Peter pulled Holly and John aside. "I need both of you to come to the sheriff's office tomorrow morning, if possible," he said.

"Sure," said Holly. "I have the contact information for the family who caused trouble with Uncle Dave at The Sapphire Pit on Monday. Do you really think they had anything to do with his death?"

"We have to cover all angles," said Peter. "And with your Uncle David, there aren't a lot of them."

With that, John yawned and rubbed his eyes. "It's been a long day, Peter. I need to hit the sack. Do you need anything else from me?"

"No. Get some rest. If I think of anything, I know where to find you."

As John turned to leave, Peter said, "Wait. Did you say you and David have a third brother?"

"Alfred. He's coming home."

Peter started to ask about Alfred but could see exhaustion overtaking John. "We'll chat more tomorrow," he said.

9

THE NEXT MORNING, gathered in the sheriff's office, Holly handed Travis the sapphire tour questionnaire and liability release form filled out by the unpleasant Missoula family.

"Ralph and Olga Jensen and their delightful son, Sebastian, aka Billy," read Travis. "He's a dentist and she's a housewife. You should have a check-off box under children for 'Brat'."

Holly laughed. "He was special, wasn't he."

"Flip a coin," Peter said to Angus and Tom. "One of you gets the privilege of driving over to Missoula to interview the Jensen family."

Tom took a coin out of his pocket. "Call it," he said.

"Heads," called Angus as Tom flipped the coin. He caught it in his hand.

"Heads. I guess you're the lucky guy, Angus."

"Dang it," said Angus. "When do you want me to go over, Peter?"

"Tomorrow morning. You don't need to check in here first. I'll clear it with Missoula County. Travis, fill him in on the incident."

Peter led Holly and John into his office and showed them the paperwork from Bob Dahl's place.

"I'm assuming you're both familiar with these." He held up the land plats, covenant list, and Last Will and Testament of Charles Anderson. "I really need some insight and explanation of the whole family dynamics. And how does Bob Dahl fit into things?"

Holly looked at John. "You know it all better than I do, Dad," she said. "I didn't even know we were related to Bob Dahl."

"We'd better get comfortable," said John. "It's a long story."

Rather than wait for his electric teapot to heat, Peter placed bags of Earl Grey into three cups of water and brought them out to boil in the micro-wave. Holly and John sank into the overstuffed leather guest chairs. When they were settled in with their tea, John began.

"Charles Anderson was my great grandfather. He was ambitious, hardworking . . . a brilliant businessman. He became very wealthy." John stopped his narrative to sip tea and contemplate the rest of his story.

"Back then, when mining was booming and Anderson was a young town, there were a lot of undesirable characters moving into the county. Many of them had no intention of working hard for a living. They came to rob and cheat as many people as they could to fill their own pockets. Old Charlie realized the Anderson family name was associated with great wealth and he needed to protect his family from crooks. Some of the family thought it was about control. I don't think so. I think he was trying to protect as many generations as he could, not only from outsiders, but also from future heirs who might lack the work ethics of that generation. Charlie had two sons and a daughter. The sons were as hard working and ambitious as Charlie. The daughter, Clara, was a renegade. At one point, she moved to Anderson as a saloon girl. When Charlie cut her off financially, she opened a brothel. Easy money in her mind. She never did marry but gave birth to an illegitimate daughter. Bob Dahl is part of that family tree. In spite of her rebellious behavior, Charlie loved his daughter and made sure she and her children would be taken care of in the future."

"So, how did he plan to protect his family?" asked Peter.

"The first thing he did was stop using the Anderson name. The name set a person up as a target for crooks, so Charlie encouraged the tradition of children using their middle names in place of Anderson. Clara dropped Anderson when she moved into town. She went by Clara Belle, so protected herself in spite of herself. That tradition still carries on today. I only started using Anderson again after I quit preaching and moved onto the mountain with the sheep. If you look in the church directory, you'll find me listed as Reverend John James."

He looked at Holly and smiled. "Holly is an Anderson, but, as you know, she goes by Holly Noelle . . . a bit cutesy for me, but that's what you get for being born on Christmas Day."

"Bob's middle name is Dahl?" asked Peter.

"No," said John, "Bob never was an Anderson. Clara's daughter had a daughter, who married a Dahl. Bob's branch of the family reverted to traditional last names."

Peter stood up, walked over to the table of papers, selected a few, and handed them to John. "Can you explain these to me?"

John took a few moments to look over the papers.

"These are land plats of property along the highway going past Anderson. They show ownership by Bob Dahl and David. I know Bob inherited the property on the east side closest to Anderson, because he was a direct descendant of Clara, and she owned that property."

"This is prime real estate. Bob was always struggling financially. Why didn't he sell it?"

"He couldn't. Charlie put it in his will that only direct descendants could inherit Anderson land and it could only be sold by a direct descendant to a direct descendant. It can't be subdivided. The first born of any branch inherits first. If there are no children, the first born of the next closest, oldest relative will inherit. David, being the oldest of three sons, inherited from our father. I was second oldest. David had no children so Holly, being my only child, will inherit everything from him."

"Did you know this, Holly?" asked Peter.

"Uncle Dave always said I was the daughter he never had. He told me I would get his house when he died. Beyond that, no."

"There's a lot more than that," said John.

Holly looked surprised. "Really?"

"Yes. I don't think you realize how big the Anderson fortune is, even divided through several generations. Outside of inheriting land, the remaining wealth is held in trusts. Not just the first born gets a piece of that, and we keep adding to it."

Peter was watching Holly. He needed to keep his personal feelings from clouding his judgement. As the sole heir to David Howard's fortune, and possible baker of a poisonous pie, she was a suspect in his murder. "Were there other covenants?" he asked.

"Beyond what was designated for the Anderson township, the rest of the land can't be developed. It can only be used by the Anderson family for farming, ranching, or mining. An Anderson can build a house or other buildings as needed, but nothing besides private use."

"That explains why there aren't businesses along the highway," said Peter.

"And why Anderson has never grown," said John. "Charlie was a smart man, but he would only acknowledge Anderson as a part of the ranch business. He couldn't see it as a separate community. The covenants also restrict certain development on property within town boundaries. Charlie wanted to make sure the town bearing his name retained a certain amount of class."

"But didn't Clara run a brothel?" asked Holly.

"Ah . . . good question. Charlie made a deal with her. If she agreed to leave the saloon, he would build her a fancy hotel to run."

"The Clara Hotel!" exclaimed Holly. "That was hers!"

"Yep. And the beauty salon and barber shop on the ground floor were hers, too. Charlie built her three businesses in one building. What he didn't know was that she added a fourth, a parlor house."

"What's that?" asked Peter.

"A fancy name for a high-class bordello," replied John. "Clara recruited the best of the local working girls and brought in a beautician from Boston to train them in the latest hair and makeup techniques. They each had a suite in the back of the hotel. The barber was Clara's long-time beau, Walter Conlin. Men who were looking for more than a haircut picked out the girl he was interested in from the salon. Walter directed him to the correct room number and the client went up the back stairs to wait for her in her sitting room."

"But I've been in that salon," said Holly. "There's a solid wall between the salon and the barber shop. How could the men see the women?"

John smiled. "Next time you're in there, take a closer look at those square wooden inserts at about eye-level in the wall. They're sliding panels. The handle is on the barbershop side."

"Wow!" said Holly, surprised.

"How did the men know which women were available?" asked Peter.

"Clara's girls wore an emerald-green bow in their hair. The salon was called The Emerald back then, too. It was her favorite color. Of course, the girls had regulars who asked for them by name."

"How do you know so much about all this?"

John grinned. "Because I am in possession of Clara's very-detailed diary. It helps pass the time while babysitting sheep in the wilderness."

A lull in the conversation left the three of them lost in their respective contemplations.

"I suppose David's house is off-limits, Peter?" John asked.

"For the time being, until our investigation is through."

"In that case, I need to look over paperwork at Holly's and then would like to visit some old friends. I'll meet you back at your house later, Holly?"

"I'll come with you, Dad," said Holly as she stood to leave.

Peter stopped her. "I need to ask you a few more questions, Holly."

"But Dad's staying at my house," grumbled Holly. "And I'm tired of all this questioning."

"Just a few questions. Give him your keys."

"It's not locked, Dad," she said to John. "I'll be there soon."

Holly slumped back into her chair with a sigh and gave Peter a less than delighted look.

"What?" she asked.

Peter put on his cop face. "Where were you on Monday night between the hours of eight and midnight?"

"What?"

"Where were you on Monday night between the hours of eight and midnight?"

"You think I murdered Uncle Dave?"

"Please just answer the question," said Peter, trying not to see the hurt and anger in her face.

"I was home. Alone. No witnesses. No alibi. Are you going to arrest me for being pathetic?"

"Do you have any proof you were home alone at that time?"

"Not unless you can trace my lame TV binge watching."

"I'll check into it. What were you watching?"

"Why does it matter?"

"Humor me."

"A documentary on the geological formation of the Grand Canyon."

"Fascinating."

"You used to think geology was fascinating."

"I used to think you were fascinating. I tolerated geology."

"So, you were faking our relationship? How long was that going on? Were we really high school sweethearts or were you faking it back then, too?" Holly's jaw clenched in anger.

"High school was different. You were different." Peter felt his last grasp on Holly slipping away.

"How was I different?"

"In high school you loved me unconditionally. In college you tried to make me into who you wanted me to be. I'm a lawman, not a geologist."

Voice raised, Holly said, "You're only a lawman because you had an absurd notion you could solve your parent's murder if you went to the police academy."

Holly stood and pushed away her chair, ready to bolt. Travis poked his head in the door. Peter, heart aching from the gibe, motioned him away.

"Sit down, Holly. We're not through."

Holly hesitated but dropped into her chair.

"How do you reimburse David for his help at The Sapphire Pit?" Peter asked.

"What does that have to do with anything?"

"Just answer the question."

"He volunteers. He gets a lunch and a bucket of dirt from the mine." Holly was angry and near to tears.

"Have you ever given him thank you gifts?"

"Gifts? Like what?"

"Just answer the question."

"No. I give him a Christmas gift every year."

"Do you ever bake for him?"

"Have you lost your mind?"

"I'm asking the questions. Do you ever bake for him?"

"Have you ever known me to bake anything?"

"Is that a no?"

"No. I mean yes, that's a no. I don't bake."

"You've never baked a pie?"

Holly looked at him incredulously. "No. I don't bake, Peter. Never."

"Have you ever bought baked goods and given them to David?"

"No. I mean, yes. I bring store-bought pie to Thanksgiving dinner."

"Anything recently?"

"No!!!"

Peter opened his desk drawer and pulled out the note from the poisoned pie. He handed it to Holly.

"Have you ever seen this before?"

Holly opened and read the note. Her eyes widened. "I didn't write this, Peter. It isn't even my handwriting."

"I know, Holly. That note was under a pie tin in David's house. The pie looked homemade, and it was possibly poisoned. We're waiting for lab results."

"Poisoned? But he was hung."

"Dr. Hamm thinks he was poisoned first. We're also waiting for toxicology reports on his stomach contents."

"Someone poisoned him and then hung him? And you thought I did it?!"

Holly was becoming hysterical. She looked down at her hand in horror and dropped the note.

"Now you have my fingerprints on the note. Are you trying to frame me?"

"No, Holly. We don't believe you did anything wrong. I had to do the official interview in case anyone ever questions the professionalism of the investigation. Because of our history."

He stood, walked around his desk, and pulled her up into his arms.

"I'm sorry I put you through that. Are you okay to drive yourself home?"

"I'm fine," she said as she pushed him away and walked out.

Peter sighed and his heart hurt. And his head hurt. He rubbed temples until the pain stopped, picked up the phone and punched Travis's line.

"Yeah, Boss?"

"Did you find any prints on those Sam Geary letters or that Winston Hayes business card?"

"Yes, we did. Along with your prints on the corner of the business card, which we could rule out with what we have on file, there are prints from two other people. One has whorls and the other has loops."

"I'm guessing Winston Hayes and Clay Pidgen. How about the letters?"

"All kinds of prints on those. We need to get prints for Clay, Winston, Sam, and Seth to rule out whose are whose."

"Winston may be troublesome. Clay and Seth should be easy. I'll work on those and also ask Dr. Hamm if we can get prints from Sam's body."

"Great. Thanks, Boss."

"Did you have any luck tracing calls to Sam's phone?"

"He didn't have it on him, and Helen didn't find it in his delivery truck. Whoever knocked him on the head and stuffed him in the mixer must have taken it."

"Did you check to see if Mary has access?"

"She is still using a phone with a curly cord leashing it to the wall. She doesn't know anything about Sam's cell phone and her name isn't on the contract."

"Okay. Good work."

Peter grabbed his keys, whistled to Zack, and readied himself for another uncomfortable visit to the Geary place. Interrupting a family making funeral plans was a close second to breaking the news of the death to the family.

He found Mary alone on the front porch, one foot prodding a hanging swing into a slow swaying arc.

"Hello, Peter. I hope you're here with better news than you had on your last visit."

"Hello, Mary," said Peter as he climbed the porch steps.

Mary patted the cushion next to her. "Sit with me, Peter. Sam and I used to sit here every morning and drink our coffee. I do miss him."

Peter sat. He and Mary swayed in silence for several minutes, Peter letting Mary set the pace of conversation.

"Tell me what you need to tell me," she said.

"No bad news today, Mary. I need help with the investigation."

"Whatever you need to find Sam's murderer."

"All I need are your fingerprints . . . and Seth's so we can eliminate them from the suspect pool."

"Sure. Seth is in the barn. I'll give him a call." She stood, the stiffness and pain of arthritis evident. "Come into the kitchen. I'll make you a cup of tea. Are you up for fresh apple cobbler?"

"Definitely!"

Mary put the teapot on to boil and made the phone call to Seth, asking him to come to the house.

"Now show me how this fingerprint stuff works."

Peter prepared his kit and gently rolled Mary's fingertips on a fingerprint card, careful not to put too much pressure on her swollen joints.

"Afternoon, Peter," said Seth as he walked in, letting the screen door slam behind him.

"My days of crime are over, Seth," said Mary. "The coppers have my prints now."

Seth gave his mother a gentle squeeze. "I suppose you need mine, too. Can't you take them off the letters?"

"It's to eliminate yours from anyone else on those letters, Seth."

"Please don't give Peter a hard time, Seth. He's doing this for us . . . and your father."

"Let's get it over with then." Seth held out his hands.

Peter thanked Mary and Seth for their help and drove to his next stop.

Clay Pigeon was not so obliging.

"I don't see why you need my fingerprints, Sheriff. I'm just the foreman. I don't have any arguments with the Gearys."

"This is so we can rule out your prints on the business card, Clay."

"But won't my prints be in the system now?"

"Only in our files in the sheriff's office. If you don't commit any crimes, you have nothing to worry about."

"Still. I don't like it."

"I can get a warrant, but I'd rather do this amicably."

Clay grumbled but held out his hands. "Okay. Get it over with."

Peter took several tries to get un-smudged prints from Clay. Consent and cooperation are two different things. Back in his Explorer, he punched in the number for Dr. Hamm.

"Hey, Doc, I need fingerprints from Sam Geary. Do you still have him in the morgue?"

"No. He's over at the funeral home. I'm not sure when the funeral is scheduled, but there are no plans for cremation, so you still have time."

"Thanks, Doc."

Peter drove slower than usual on his way to the funeral home. In his mind's eye, he could still see Sam Geary's lifeless green eyes staring at him from out of the mixer bowl. On a positive note, in the funeral parlor Sam's body would lie out for viewing and those eyes would be sewn closed.

The Gateway to Eternal Rest funeral parlor was conveniently located on a side street around the corner from the Stone County Hospital. In the alley behind the hospital, a cement ramp led the way to a set of double doors opening into the basement morgue. Bodies were easily transferred on gurneys from the morgue to a ramp and then through a set of double doors leading into the basement processing room of the mortuary. In a fit of poor taste or tasteless humor, the double doors leading to the processing room were painted to look like the golden gateway to heaven. Peter chose to enter through the front door and be led down to the basement by the mortician as there was less chance of walking in on the processing of a body.

The acidic stink of embalming fluid invaded Peter's nostrils as soon as he walked through the door. He was met by mortician Lee Garnet, dressed as ever in an immaculate black suit and garnet red tie. Peter was tempted at times to knock on Lee's door in the wee hours of the morning to see if he slept in that suit.

"Good to see you, Sheriff," said Lee, extending his hand.

"You, too, Lee. I'm here on the Sam Geary case."

"Interesting. What can I do for you?"

Peter handed Lee paperwork giving him permission to obtain fingerprints from Sam Geary's corpse.

"Everything seems to be in order," said Lee, flipping through the papers and verifying the signature. "Follow me."

The stairway to the processing room was behind a locked door to prevent a grieving loved one from accidently walking in on an embalming. The stench of death and preservation became worse as they made their way down the stairs. Peter coughed several times in an attempt to stop gagging. Lee stopped suddenly on the way down, causing Peter to bump into him.

"I am so sorry, Peter. I sometimes forget how much the odors can affect those not accustomed to embalming."

Lee reached into a suit pocket and pulled out a small container of medicinal vapor rub. He handed it to Peter.

"Here. Dab a little of that under your nose."

Peter did as told and was surprised at the difference. The strong odor of the rub covered up the offensive odor of the processing room. *I guess sometimes you can put perfume on a pig,* he thought.

Only one body occupied the processing room. Peter would rather have had the face covered, but it was necessary for him to verify it was Sam Geary before he took the fingerprints. Seeing Sam's body laid out on the embalming table with his appendages in all the right places and his eyes closed as if in sleep helped erase the horror of the murder scene from Peter's mind. He laid out his fingerprinting equipment on a side table and quickly completed his task. He conveyed his thanks to Lee, made a hasty retreat through the golden gated back door, and returned to deposit his cache of fingerprint cards into his locked desk drawer.

Each season has its charm, but a common regret among those dwelling in the mountains of Montana was too little time enjoying the warmth of its brief summers. In atonement for the sins of harsh lingering winters, nature granted long days of summer sunshine. A blue cloudless sky, acting as a backdrop to Anderson's surrounding nature, and the scent of pine lured Peter from his office. On the way out, he let Travis know he would be unreachable until morning. Swinging the always ready backpack out of his Explorer, he whistled for Zack, made his way through the streets of town and into the surrounding wilderness. A narrow rocky path wound its way upwards to the highest peak of the Moonlight Mountains. Climbing at a swift pace, Peter was soon breathing hard, clearing his mind of frustrations and his body of tensions built up over the past several days. In the morning, on his way back, he could enjoy the spring-fed stream bubbling next to the path, the wildflowers, bird song, and crisp mountain air. Today he was in need of a cleansing workout.

10

ANGUS TOOK EXTRA care preparing his uniform the next morning. Unlike most boys raised on a ranch, Angus's mom insisted he learn what men typically considered 'women's work.' Angus washed and ironed as well as any professional laundry. His uniform was spotless and stiff with starch, his shoes polished to a mirror-like gloss. He dressed and then carefully filled his duty belt with handcuffs, pepper spray, freshly charged taser, and the other necessary tools of daily life that weighed down a law enforcement officer. Today was special, a test. He was going out on an assignment to question and investigate possible murder suspects. Tom and Peter may have considered the coin toss a loss for

Angus, but he had been waiting for a chance to prove himself as a legitimate sheriff's deputy since he began working under his Uncle Jake two years previously. He was not deaf to the whispers and snickers branding him as a token 'tip of the hat' to his family's law enforcement legacy. Uncle Jake, worried about accusations of nepotism, regularly assigned Angus the most menial and least responsible tasks. Angus would not hesitate to leave Rumsey and sign on with Anderson full time if Peter would only ask. Today was a chance to prove himself worthy.

Summertime in the mountains offers many opportunities for enjoyment to those so inclined. Traveling an open road free of ice and snow, windows rolled down, old-time rock-n-roll, and summer sunshine can fill even the most churlish hearts with joy. Angus cruised into Missoula, belting out garbled lyrics and tapping his fingers to the beat. The address preloaded into his navigator, he drove with little difficulty to an older part of the city, a suburban street lined with slowly decaying post-World War II prefab split-level houses. Angus had expected more from the description of the Missoula dentist, his spoiled brat kid and bully of a wife. A sagging chain-link fence circled the easter-egg blue house with faded chipping paint. Dirt, broken toys, and a rusting bike frame filled the yard. The only hints of grass hid in the shadows under bushes and along the sides of the house. Angus parked his vehicle across the street from the front gate. He called into the sheriff's office and verified the address. Address correct. This was the dentist's house and not a popular dentist if this was all his earnings could afford.

Angus scanned the yard, looking for signs of a dog before he walked through the gate. If there was one, all the usual paraphernalia, food dishes and toys, were in the back. He closed the gate and started up the walk as a large slobbering pit bull burst through the screen door and headed straight for him. Angus grabbed at his utility belt, his hand closing around his taser. In the few seconds it took for the dog to leap for his throat, he had the taser out in front and activated. Immediately the pit bull lay twitching at his feet. Out of the house came an obese woman in a lime green Hawaiian-print muumuu, welding an aluminum baseball bat. Angus assumed she was coming to protect him from the dog until he saw the bat aimed at his head. He held his left arm up to protect his head and reached for pepper spray with his right. Pain shot through Angus's arm as it cracked under the force of the bat. At the same time, he felt teeth sink into his calf. The dog, recovered, was attacking.

"You hurt my dog, you pig," screamed the woman, taking aim for another hit with the bat.

She dropped the bat and clutched at her face as a stream of pepper spray hit her. Angus swung the can downward toward the attacking dog and sprayed again. The dog yelped and let go of his leg.

With both the woman and the dog on the ground whining, screaming, and clawing at their faces, Angus was able to take a breath and assess the situation. He was sure his arm was broken, and blood was streaming out of a wound to his leg. Thankful that he kept his cellphone in his utility belt, he called 911.

Help on its way, Angus cuffed the still screaming woman and gave the dog an extra shot of spray for good measure. He was beyond sympathy for either creature and knew his ability to stop another attack was weak. He sat on the ground with his back against the fence, wrapped the bleeding leg with a piece of cloth torn from the already destroyed pant leg, and waited.

ON ARRIVING AT the ER, a nurse washed and bandaged the wound on Angus's leg. An IV was started in his good arm for morphine and then an antibiotic to prevent bacterial infection from the dog bite.

Feeling groggy and pain-free from the morphine, Angus watched the ER doc apply a splint to his arm.

A nurse poked her head around the privacy curtain and asked if a police officer could come through and ask him a few questions.

"Fine with me," answered the doctor. He looked at Angus for approval.

"Sure," said Angus

The nurse held the curtain aside and a young-looking officer walked past her and ducked under the curtain.

"Officer Hanson," he said, introducing himself. "And you are Officer Angus McLeod of Stone County, correct?"

"Yes," replied Angus "My official assignment is in Rumsey, but I help out in Anderson quite a bit. I'm over there helping with the investigation into those murders."

"And I'm told you were cleared by the police chief here in Missoula to question the Jensens in conjunction with that investigation?"

"That's right."

He watched the doctor for a few minutes, then pulled up an extra stool.

"The dog has been euthanized and its head sent to the vet lab in Bozeman. The owners couldn't provide proof of a current rabies vaccination."

"How long will that take?"

"We'll probably have the results back tomorrow afternoon."

"Should I be worried?" asked Angus

"Rabies is usually fatal," said the doctor, "but starting you on shots now will prevent you from contracting the disease. We can't take the chance of waiting for results from the lab even if it is only tomorrow."

The doctor finished the splint and filled a syringe out of a vial.

"I'll give you the first vaccination close to the site of the bite. If the dog is negative for rabies, you won't need to finish the series. If the test comes back positive, you'll need three more shots at three, seven, and fourteen days after the bite. The nurse will set you up for those before you leave."

"Do I have to get them in my stomach?"

"No. That was a theory years ago. Studies have shown that an intramuscular injection in the arm is more effective."

His leg still numb, Angus didn't feel the shot.

Officer Hanson waited until Angus was dressed and release papers were signed.

"I'm starved," he said. "Let's get something to eat and then we'll work on getting you home."

Angus looked down at his uniform. The left leg of his once crisp and spotless uniform trousers was ripped away at the thigh. His leg was bandaged and bloody from ankle to knee. The left arm of his uniform shirt was gone, cut away by a nurse in the emergency room. A sling partially hid the splint covering his damaged arm.

"I'm a mess," he said. "If I go into a restaurant looking like this it might scare people."

"Not where we're going," said Officer Hanson. "By the way, my name is Glenn."

"Thanks for all this."

"Angus McLeod. Must be some Scottish ancestry there."

"Yeah, but that's not why the name Angus. My dad is a cattle rancher. When I was born, he took one look at my red hair and named me Angus after his favorite cattle breed. I have a blonde twin sister goes by Char, short for Charolais."

Glenn laughed. "It could be worse. He could have named you Hereford and Holstein."

"I hope my mom would have put her foot down on that. So, where is this lunch place with a lax dress code?"

"Do you like fried chicken?"

"Who doesn't!"

"The best fried chicken in the world is in a little dive off Higgins Avenue. They cater to the police crowd, so you'll be surrounded by cops. They've all had days like this."

Glenn understated the reaction at The Chicken Coop. A variety of law enforcement sat at tables eating or stood in line to order. They took one look at Angus's battered uniform and bandages, and clapped and hooted.

"Crossing guard duty at the grade school?" called a tough-looking veteran amid whoops of laughter.

Angus's face blazed, but he smiled, waved his good hand, and endured the ribbing.

After they ordered and the attention in the room went back to baskets of fried chicken, Glenn led Angus to a quiet corner table.

"I have some information on the Jensen family I thought might interest you," he said.

"Oh?"

"Ralph Jensen works in a dental lab a few blocks from here."

"I thought he was a dentist."

"Used to be. He lost his license."

"How bad do things have to be for a dentist to lose his license?" asked Angus

"Thirteen-year-old died in the chair."

"Yikes!"

"Yeah. The way I hear tell, she was a handful and he needed to pull a couple teeth. He put her under because she wouldn't hold still. He wasn't trained or licensed to use sedation, but he used it anyway. There was a big investigation and they uncovered quite a few more deaths."

"In his office? Why wasn't he caught sooner?"

"The victims were elderly with no family. Nobody to care when they died. Nobody asked questions. He passed them off as old people with bad hearts . . . that sort of thing. When the girl died, investigators picked up on the other deaths and investigated those, too. His wife, Olga, the one who attacked you, she was his office manager."

"And she knew about the deaths?"

"And covered them up by changing records."

"Was she charged?"

"Yeah, it went to court, but there wasn't enough evidence to convict. He covered for her; said she knew nothing about it. He got off with probation and lost his dental license."

"Did they always live in that rat hole?"

"No, they had a big house up Rattlesnake Canyon. After he lost his license and his business, he also lost a couple of civil suits that added up to millions of dollars. As far as I know, she hasn't worked since. They rent that place they're living in now."

"So, money is an issue."

"Yep, and both of them are capable of murder."

The men finished their lunches and made their way back to the patrol car.

"There's a highway patrolman working around Bearmouth. I'm going to drive you and your vehicle that far. A couple of deputies from Anderson will pick you up and take you the rest of the way and the hy-po will give me a ride back here."

"Sounds like a good plan," said Angus. "Thanks again for helping out."

"Hey, gets me out of crossing guard duty," Glenn said with a grin.

A SOMBER GROUP gathered around Travis's desk, Angus in his tattered uniform. The morphine was wearing off and he hadn't yet filled his prescription for pain medication. Discomfort showed in his face and caught in his voice.

"I'll help Travis with paperwork. And I can do research in the library. I'm really good on the computer. I could do ride-a-longs and interviews," pleaded Angus. "If you send me back, Jake will put me on medical leave for two months."

"It is workman's comp, Angus," said Peter. "And you have the sick leave available."

"What if Dr. Hamm releases me to work?"

"He won't. Tell you what, Tom will drive you over to the pharmacy so you can fill your prescriptions. You can stay in your apartment in Anderson. You don't have to go back to Rumsey. Give yourself the three days to rest up. If the rabies test comes back positive on that dog, you'll need to go back to

Missoula for another shot anyway. We'll work out a plan for you after that."

"Okay," said Angus reluctantly. He got to his feet, wincing in pain.

Tom followed Angus out the door and down the stairs to his Explorer. Climbing into the passenger side seat was too difficult with the left side of his body out of commission, so Angus rode in the back driver's side seat. Tom insisted on going into the pharmacy to fill the prescription. While Angus, trying to ignore the mounting pain, was waiting with the window open to the sunshine, Dr. Hamm walked past and spotted him.

"Hey, Angus, what are you doing in the back seat? Zack call dibs on the front today?"

Angus pointed to his splinted arm.

"Ouch! How'd you do that?"

Angus gave him an abbreviated version of the story.

"Ah, a classic night-stick fracture," said Dr. Hamm.

"Hey. Do you think I can get a work release?"

Dr. Hamm laughed. "Sorry. You're gonna be out for at least two months."

"Dang," said Angus.

"Make an appointment for next week. We should be able to put a cast on by then. After that we'll take an X-ray every couple weeks to keep track of healing."

"Anything I can do to make it heal faster?"

"Take calcium, magnesium, Vitamin D3, and Vitamin C. Follow the dosage instructions on the labels," said Dr. Hamm. Patients had a tendency to overdo things with the theory that if a little works, a lot will work better.

"Vitamin C?" asked Angus. "Isn't that for colds?"

"It seems to help with fracture pain. We don't really know why."

"Okay, thanks Doc."

"Take it easy and enjoy your vacation."

Angus scowled. He didn't enjoy vacations. He wasn't a reader or TV watcher. He didn't like to play tourist or hike or fish. His frugal parents didn't approve of leisure time, and he never learned how to do anything but work. That thought gave him an idea. Official or not, he would work.

Tom came out with the prescriptions, handed them to Angus and drove him to his apartment above the Moonlight Mountain Brewery.

"Thanks. Tom. Would you tell Peter that Dr. Hamm said I'll be out for a couple months?"

"Uh, sure, Angus," said Tom, surprised at the change in attitude.

"INTERESTING," SAID PETER. "It's not like Angus to give up so easily, but he was in a lot of pain."

Peter, Tom, Travis, and Helen were gathered in Peter's office going over the days' happenings.

"Did you get the toxicology lab report back?" asked Helen.

"Just this afternoon," replied Peter. "A courier dropped it by. I'm thankful for Dr. Hamm and his connections in Missoula."

"So…what did it say?" urged Travis.

"Both the pie and David's stomach contents contained lethal amounts of Atropa belladonna, aka, deadly nightshade."

"No kidding," said Tom.

"Is there any chance it could have been accidental?" asked Travis.

"Deadly nightshade can be mistaken for blueberries," added Helen. She glanced around at the sudden silence and raised eyebrows of her colleagues. "I took a class on forensic investigation of plant-based poisonings. It's more common than you think."

"But someone tried to frame Holly," said Peter. "Why would they do that if the poisoning was accidental?"

"And you're sure it wasn't Holly?" asked Tom.

"I am. Yes, Holly and I have a past, and we are still close, but I knew right away the handwriting on that note wasn't Holly's. I questioned her. I was careful to be objective," said Peter looking pointedly at Tom. "She was completely surprised the pie was poisoned."

"But she is a top suspect because she inherits everything," said Tom

"I checked that out, too. She had no idea about the inheritance or how much land and money was involved. She only knew about the house."

"So she says, and it's a pretty great house," Tom persisted, "and worth a lot."

"We'll keep her on the list," conceded Peter. He knew better than to argue with a stubborn Tom.

"She doesn't bake . . . ever," said Helen. "She would have to be in cahoots with someone else. That pie looked professional."

"Who else do we know involved with this case could have baked the pie?" asked Peter.

"Bob, obviously," said Travis. "If we assume the cases are connected."

"Bob disappears the same day David is poisoned and then strangled by hanging," said Helen. "Bob and David are connected through family and land."

"Bob had some suspicious money stuff going on," continued Travis. "First, he is barely scraping by and then he gets a whole bunch of money, remodels the bakery, and buys expensive new equipment. And there were all those calls to David."

"The loan didn't come through a bank," said Peter. "Did you have any luck tracing the money, Travis?"

"Nope. The bank didn't either, which they said was unusual. I thought about David, but I doubt he would be tech savvy enough to hide a transfer from the bank."

"I can't see dirty money coming from David, either, but people surprise you," mused Peter. He lifted four fingerprint card cases off his desk and handed them to Travis. "Here are prints for Clay Pidgen, and Seth, Mary, and Sam Geary."

"Did you have any trouble getting them?" asked Travis.

"Not from Seth and Mary. Clay was a little owly. He may have something in his past he's worried about. Sam was completely cooperative."

"Hasn't Clay been around here his whole life?" asked Helen. "I don't remember hearing about him being involved in anything questionable."

"Me neither," said Peter. "But it might not be something that happened around here."

"Any ideas how to get ahold of prints for Winston Hayes?" asked Travis.

"Not yet. Angus did say he called the airports in Connecticut and there are no records of Mr. Hayes flying to Montana or anywhere else in the last couple months. Work on that business card. Any prints that aren't mine or Clay's will most likely belong to Winston Hayes. We can run them through IAGFIS and maybe we'll get lucky."

"Sounds good."

"Anything interesting happening around town?" asked Peter

"Just the usual. A few speeders, a few drunk tourists at the brewery, cows on the road. Fairly quiet," reported Tom.

"Good," said Peter. "With Angus out for two months, we won't have any back-up. Quiet is better."

"What are we going to do about the Missoula angle?" asked Helen.

"Let Missoula handle it for now," replied Peter. "They're on board since Olga assaulted Angus. Anything else?" he asked, anxious for the day to be done.

Helen smiled. "Hiking back into the cabin tonight?" she asked.

"Yeah," said Peter. His phone buzzed on his desk. He turned and glanced at the caller displayed. Linda.

"Hey, Linda."

"Hi Pete. We have a steak with your name on it ready for the barbecue and Cold Smoke in the fridge."

Peter hesitated, but not long enough for Linda to notice.

"That's great, Linda. When should I be over?"

"As soon as you can get away from the office."

"I have to make a quick phone call first and then I'll head over. See you soon."

"Bummer," said Helen.

"That's okay. I'll hike up tomorrow. Can't turn down a free steak dinner with my favorite brother."

"Only brother," laughed Helen.

Peter regretted missing the hike. He needed the workout and that was the best time to mull over cases. Townspeople were beginning to ask him when he was going to solve the murders . . . and what happened to Bob?

After Helen left, he picked up the phone and punched in the number for Jake McLeod, sheriff of Deer Lodge County and Angus's official boss.

"Jake, here."

"Hi, Jake. This is Peter."

"Hey, Peter. Are you about finished with my deputy? Things are getting busy here. I could use his help."

"That's what I'm calling about, Jake. Angus was involved in an altercation during a routine inquiry today. He's going to be out on medical leave for a couple months."

"What?! Leave it to that knucklehead to get hurt when I need him."

"He's going to be okay, by the way."

"Whatever. Send him home when he's healed up. I don't want to see him before then . . . and keep this under your hat. This kind of thing could hurt my . . . uh, I mean, the department's reputation."

Linda, Paul, and Peter settled in deck chairs, the irresistible aroma of steak and mesquite emanating from the grill. Peter sipped from a cold can of his favorite beer, thoughts of the hour-long hike to his cabin completely forgotten.

"Well," said Linda eagerly. "Fill us in. What's new with the murders?"

Paul rolled his eyes. "You are such a ghoul."

Peter laughed, then told them about the poisoned pie, and Angus's confrontation with the Jensen family in Missoula.

"Poor Angus," said Linda. "I'll have the church ladies get some food ready to bring over to him. Several frozen casseroles and lots of baked goods should keep him going and his spirits up."

"I'm sure he'll appreciate that, Linda. Thank you."

"Do you really think that nutty family had anything to do with David's murder?" asked Paul.

"Hard to tell," replied Peter. "The only connection with David is that episode at The Sapphire Pit, but someone poisoned him, and someone hung him and not necessarily the same someone."

"Considering Olga Jenson's reaction to Angus, I'd say she's high on the suspect list," said Paul.

"I was surprised you let Barb leave town with the investigation still going on," said Linda

"I didn't. She was supposed to check in with us if she left town. Where did she go?"

"I don't know. I've been trying to call her for the last few days to see if she needed anything. She doesn't answer her phone. I drove past the house yesterday and again today. The car is gone."

"Shoot," said Peter "I'll need to get a warrant to search the house and put out an APB on the car. Did she say anything to you about leaving?"

"Not a thing. She may have gone to Missoula to stay with her son and daughter-in-law, Sally's parents."

Peter sighed. "I've been so busy with everything else; I didn't notice she wasn't pestering me about Bob."

"Do you think he's still alive?" asked Paul.

"No idea."

11

ANGUS WOKE EARLY the next morning, stiff, sore, and irritable. Painkillers and exhaustion from the day before kept him asleep for twelve hours straight, which annoyed him. The stiffness and pain annoyed him. He was mostly annoyed because all those things proved everyone right who said he wouldn't be able to go back to work. But he had a plan. Angus was not well known among the locals of Anderson. He mostly helped out during busy tourist events, outdoor concerts, Fourth of July celebrations, that sort of thing. A bright red stubble covered his face where he needed a shave. He would let it grow. The beard, mustache, messy hair, shorts, T-shirt, and sandals of a Missoula yuppie playing tree hugger was the only disguise he would need. But first, he would talk to one of the locals he did know well. Holly.

Angus popped a couple more painkillers and the prescribed antibiotics. He planned to pick up the vitamins Dr. Hamm recommended after his talk with Holly. He stuck his splinted arm in an old plastic bread bag, checking first for holes, and slipped a large rubber band around the opening to keep out water. He needed a shower.

Gazing out the window of his apartment above the brewery, showered and dressed, Angus contemplated his options. Anderson, like most Montana mining towns, was built on the side of a mountain. The ER doctor told him to stay off his leg and keep it elevated. Walking on level roads wasn't an option, the steep rocky streets of Anderson even less so. Laughter and bits of conversation from people gathered at sidewalk tables bubbled through the open window, along with sounds of passing cars. He envied their freedom. Across the street was a cluster of women sifting through sidewalk sale clothing racks. Angus recognized them as locals and among them was Lorene Hamm, the doctor's wife. Unlike the pastor's wife, Lorene didn't have church and community obligations sucking up her time, but she did have a strong sense of goodwill and Angus had her cell number saved from past events.

Angus found Lorene Hamm in his contacts and hit the phone icon. He watched her fumble in her purse, pull out her cellphone and swipe 'answer'.

"Hello?"

"Hi, Mrs. Hamm. This is Angus McLeod."

"Oh, hi, Angus. I hear you're a little banged up."

"Yeah, dang it. A broken arm and a nasty dog bite on my leg. I'm out on sick leave for two months."

"Bummer. Boring for you and I know that Peter and the gang at the sheriff's office will be missing you."

"Yeah."

"So, what can I do for you Angus?"

"Dr. Hamm said I need to keep off my leg. No walking except to take care of myself, and I can't drive because of my arm. I was wondering if you would have time to take me on a couple quick errands today. It wouldn't take long," he added.

"Where are you?"

"In the apartment above the brewery."

She looked up, saw him in the window, and laughed. He waved.

"Sure, Angus. Do you need to go now?"

"No. Whenever it's convenient for you. I need to stop at the pharmacy and grocery store and also wanted to drop something off at The Sapphire Pit for Holly. She won't be down from the mountain until early afternoon."

"I'll pick you up at two."

"Thanks. I really appreciate it."

"You're welcome. Bye now."

His first hurdle out of the way, Angus needed to work on a cover for visiting Holly. What could he possibly need to drop off to her? He rummaged around in the bedroom closet and found a gift bag left over from a past community event. Decorated in multi-colored stripes and a big orange bow, it was neutral enough not to insinuate a birthday or holiday. His hope was that Lorene wouldn't ask. The bag still contained unused and long expired local store coupons. He tossed those in the trash. Before the Missoula incident, Angus had bought a small box of fudge from the candy store for his mom's birthday. She would be just as happy with flowers. Angus found a tablet and pen and wrote a note for Holly.

> *I need to talk to you about a case I'm working on. Just between us please. I'm not on duty but staying in town so call anytime.*

He added his phone number and dropped the note and the box of fudge into the gift bag. Perfect.

Angus made his way slowly and painfully down the narrow stairway leading to Main Street. He was overdue for a pain pill, but they made him drowsy, and he wanted to be wide awake for his meeting with Holly. When Lorene pulled up in front of the brewery, he was sitting at a sidewalk table, enjoying the afternoon sun. In spite of the pleasant weather, his face was pale and strained.

"Are you sure you're up to this?" asked Lorene, as he settled into the passenger seat.

"I'll be okay," he said. "After this I won't need to go out for a while."

"You know," she said, "Linda Elliott has the church ladies cooking and baking all kinds of casseroles and goodies for you. You shouldn't need much food."

"Really? Wow, that's really nice. Do they even know me?"

"Linda is Peter's sister-in-law. I'm sure he's mentioned you and told them about the attack."

Lorene insisted on carrying the shopping basket for Angus as he made his way up and down aisles choosing fresh items like fruit and yogurt to supplement the anticipated casseroles. They checked out with only one paper sack of groceries, which Lorene insisted on carrying.

"I really appreciate this, Mrs. Hamm," said Angus, feeling like he was a kid again, shopping with his mom.

"It's no problem at all, Angus, but I insist that you stay in the car and let me go into the pharmacy for you. You're pale as a ghost and so shaky you can hardly hold onto your wallet."

In the car, she handed him a small notebook and pen out of the console.

"Now, write out what you need, and I'll go in and get it. And then we'll go to The Sapphire Pit, and I'll bring that pretty yellow bag to Holly. You don't want her seeing you like this anyway if you're trying to make a good impression."

Angus blushed as red as his beard.

"And I won't say a word to anyone," she said and gave him a wink.

<hr>

EXHAUSTED FROM HIS busy morning, Angus struggled to climb the stairs to his apartment. Lorene recruited Bud Henderson, owner of the brewery, to assist. Bud was big enough to toss Angus over his shoulders and carry him up the stairs, but in deference to Angus's injuries and pride, Bud grasped him around the waist and hauled him up that way. Bud made sure Angus was settled in his easy chair and had everything he needed including Bud's phone number for future assists. Angus was asleep before the latch closed on his apartment door and didn't wake until his phone began buzzing several hours later.

"Hullo," answered a groggy Angus.

"Hi, Angus. This is Holly. Did I wake you up?"

"Um, yeah," said Angus, struggling upright. "But that's okay. Time for me to be up anyway."

"You said you needed to talk to me about something. I'm done at The Sapphire Pit for the day. Did you want to meet me somewhere?"

Angus looked at his swollen leg and arm splint. He felt exhausted even after his nap.

"I'm kind of banged up and probably overdid things this morning already. Can you come over here? We can order takeout from the brewery. They make an excellent bison burger."

"That sounds great, actually. I haven't had a brewery burger in ages. On my way."

Angus called the brewery and ordered two Bison Burgers with onion rings and a growler of the house special. The brewery didn't normally have a delivery service, but he played the pity card and asked the bartender if it could be delivered upstairs.

"Sure Angus. I heard you were banged up. Anything to support our hard-working law enforcement."

"Thanks. I really appreciate it."

Holly and the food arrived together. The flurry of paying the bill, thanking and tipping the barmaid, and digging into the food bags to appease their hunger dispersed any awkwardness Holly and Angus may have felt over their unusual meeting. Angus was grateful when Holly's asking about his injuries opened the door for the questions he wanted to ask her.

"I heard you were in Missoula questioning that rude Jensen family about Uncle Dave's murder when you got hurt."

"Yeah. I didn't get any questioning done. Olga and her pit bull attacked before I got to the door."

"What were you going to ask her?"

"Just the usual. 'Where were you Monday night between eight and midnight?' That kind of stuff. The thing is, after everything happened and I was in the emergency room, an officer from the Missoula police department came to question me. Nice guy."

Angus told Holly about his lunch with Glenn Hanson and what he had learned about the Jensen family.

"Wow! They were unpleasant people, but I didn't expect that," she said.

"How big was that sapphire they tried to take from David?" asked Angus.

"Significant in size, maybe three carats. Depending on color and clarity, and lack of inclusions, it could be worth thousands."

"Would David have known that?"

"Definitely. Dave was an expert. He's been doing this his entire life. He supplemented his apparently immense wealth selling sapphires he found at the sapphire mine."

"You had no idea how wealthy he was?"

"No! Absolutely not! Are you going to accuse me of his murder, too?"

Angus's stomach lurched. He finally had Holly all to himself, was on the verge of forming a partnership, and now she was angry and standing to leave. And why was she so defensive about the whole thing?

"No, Holly. No. What do you mean? Are people blaming you for David's death? Please don't leave. I don't think you're a murderer."

Holly looked at him suspiciously but returned to her chair.

"Peter actually questioned me like I was a suspect. It was humiliating." She sobbed.

"I'm sure he didn't mean anything by it," said Angus. "In his job he has to stay neutral and not let personal feelings cloud his judgement."

"That's what he said."

"I never considered you as a suspect. In fact, I invited you over tonight because I'm on leave for two months while I heal from these injuries. I want to keep investigating unofficially . . . just to keep from getting bored. Nobody knows David and sapphires as well as you. If talking about it makes you feel uncomfortable or puts you in bad position with Peter, we don't have to."

Holly's body relaxed and she smiled. "Okay. It might be fun to play amateur sleuth. All those Nancy Drew mysteries I read should come in handy."

Relieved, Angus chewed and swallowed several bites of bison burger. "Do you know if anything was missing from David's house? Was that sapphire still there?" he asked.

"I don't know. Peter didn't say anything about a robbery."

"Could you look?"

"Hmmmm. Dave has a room off the kitchen. It used to be the pantry. He turned it into a workshop where he cleaned and cut sapphires. I'll tell Peter I need something in there. I don't want to try and sneak in and get caught. He'll really suspect me then."

"Deal," said Angus. "Thanks!"

They finished their meal and the growler of beer, laughing and telling stories of local characters and small-town life. Angus was smitten and Holly was tipsy.

"I don't think you should drive home," said Angus. "Can your dad come and get you?"

"I called when you were in the bathroom. He's on his way."

John's signature footsteps echoed through the hallway followed by a solid knock on the door.

"He's here," announced Angus, sad to have the evening come to an end.

Holly gave him a sideways hug and thanked him for dinner. She winked and said she would be chatting with him soon.

Seeing the wink, John thought, *First Matthew and now Angus. Peter better get his rear in gear or he's going to lose her.*

12

"**D**ID YOU AT least catch your limit before you caught yourself?" asked Dr. Hamm as he made a loop out of seventeen-pound monofilament and slipped it over and into the bend of the hook protruding from Peter's right nostril.

"Just enough to pay my doctor bill."

"Those are nice looking trout," Doc said as he used his left hand to put pressure on the eye of the hook to release the barb embedded in Peter's skin.

A quick, but firm jerk on the monofilament brought the hook out.

"Gee, not even a one, two, three count down today?" asked Peter, rubbing his nose.

"We've been through this too many times. You're on to me. Hold still while I disinfect the wound." He applied Hibiclens with a sterile sponge swab. "You should have refills left on your antibiotic prescription."

"I do. It's good through the end of the year. Thanks, Doc."

Lorene reached over Peter's shoulder and set a steaming plate of biscuits and gravy in front of him. "Home visits get a free breakfast. Just don't tell the rest of his patients."

"She's softening you in hopes you'll tell her your fishing secrets," said Doc.

Peter grinned. "Old family recipe. I'm sworn to secrecy."

In reality, fly fishing was an art Peter could not master. He barely managed the fundamentals, but not for lack of trying. Building on years of indulgent instruction, first by his father and then the Stone County sheriff who took over after his father's death, Peter watched videos and read books and knew the lessons by heart.

Pace. Pause. Ten and two. Let your rod do the work.

He knew all the knots—the perfection loop, surgeons knot, nail knot, clinch knot—but his big fingers struggled to hold the lines and leaders. He was too proud to ask for help.

The desire to tie flies came from his mother. Always one to find her own path, she rejected fly tying norms and invented her own. Out of that creative quirkiness came a dry fly that made no sense but could not fail. Peter spent the evening hours in his cabin bent over a vise and hook, wrapping hackle and dubbing into thread to form her special fly. She called it the Magic ET because it resembled no earthly insect. It was the only fly Peter tied and the only fly he used.

A small shallow lake on Peter's property, formed as a mountain stream passed through a narrow meadow, was home to a healthy population of Montana's native cutthroat trout. Most importantly, it was secluded enough that there were no witnesses to Peter's dismal attempts at casting. Abandoned flies decorated the upper reaches of surrounding trees and bushes. Lake water, grass stains, and mud covered his shorts and legs, a result of tripping over his own line. Every now and then, he would get it right and the ET would work its magic. Thumb on top, fly in the water, tip down, the perfect roll cast. The irresistible Magic ET skims the surface and the fish bites. Rarely did he walk down the trail toward town without a creel full of trout.

13

PETER, REFRESHED FROM a restful weekend on the mountain and energized from his hike back to town and a hearty breakfast compliments of Lorene Hamm, walked into the sheriff's office ready to tackle whatever the day might bring. Zack, who spent his hike down the mountain chasing rabbits and squirrels, lay panting by the window, while Peter sat at his desk letting a weekend full of voice messages play back.

"Missoula County sheriff on line one," said Travis through the intercom.

Peter picked up the line. "This is Peter."

"Hey, Peter. This is Nick Patterson."

"Hey Nick. How are things in Missoula County?"

"Always something, but we're holding our own. I heard a rumor one of your deputies wandered across the county line and got himself beat up."

"Yeah. Routine digging into a murder, and he hit a live wire. He'll be out a couple months, but he'll be okay."

"What are the damages?"

"Nasty dog bite and a broken arm, compliments of the owner."

"I'm told the dog got put down and the owner's in jail."

"Right where they both should be."

"Would your murder investigation have anything to do with the stomach samples your coroner sent into the crime lab last week?"

"Uh, yeah. Why?" asked Peter, swinging his legs off his desk, suddenly alert.

"Interesting coincidence. Tuesday, we got a call from the truck stop outside Clinton. A customer pulled into the side parking lot next to another vehicle. The windows were open so she could see the driver. He looked like he was sleeping. She didn't think much of it, until she came back out, took a closer look, and thought he looked odd; eyes half open, head at an awkward angle, vomit down the front of his shirt. She went back in and got the cashier. Cashier went out, tried to wake the guy and realized he was dead."

"Not picking up on the coincidence."

"Yada yada yada, the coroner did an autopsy, ruled out all the usuals like heart attack, sent the stomach contents into the crime lab and it comes back as deadly nightshade poisoning via pie. Sound familiar?"

Stunned, it took Peter a few moments to collect his thoughts.

"Any idea where he got the pie?"

"Same cashier remembers him coming in and buying a large coffee. No pie. In the truck we found a paper towel with most of a pie crust and some filling. He either didn't like the crust or started feeling sick before he finished. We're thinking he came across the pie somewhere, possibly in a house in Anderson, and wrapped a piece up for later."

"Holy cow," said Peter. "Do you have an ID on the guy?"

"That's an interesting story, too. The guy had no ID on him. Nothing. Not even a credit card. But plenty of cash in his wallet and more in the glove box. We're talking tens of thousands. There were also several guns with ammo."

"Gun trace?"

"No serial numbers. They were removed, and not by amateurs. The crime lab couldn't lift the numbers."

"What about the vehicle?"

"Plates registered under a corporation in Washington State, BBR Inc. It was a dead end past that."

"Fingerprints?"

Nick grinned. "Here's where it gets really interesting. His prints set off lights and sirens all over the place, linked to several aliases and crime going back decades, everything from armed robbery to assault to extortion starting when he was a juvenile. Original name believed to be Feliks Petrov."

"Sounds foreign."

"Russian. The crime lab is confirming the stomach contents from your Mr. Howard and Feliks came from the same pie. If you can bring us the roll of paper towels from Mr. Howard's house, we can possibly confirm Feliks's paper towel came from the same roll."

"So, what is a Russian thug from Washington State doing in Anderson, stealing poisonous pie and possibly murdering a nice old man?"

"Good question. Have you ever heard of the Russian mafia?"

"Uh, maybe, kind of rings a bell."

"Like the Italian mafia and just as brutal. Known primarily as Bratva, there are thousands of groups throughout the US. Supposedly this bunch in Washington State control the city of Seattle."

"Had no idea. I seem to be saying that a lot lately."

"Can you think of any reason the Russian mafia would want to murder a nice old man in Anderson?"

"Or a baker," mused Peter.

"Huh?"

"The other murder was a dairyman on his early-morning delivery route. He was murdered in the local bakery. The baker is nowhere to be found. The dairyman had separate issues with the baker and another unknown. We're trying to sort out if he was a target or mistaken for the baker."

"Nothing boring in Anderson, is there? Still doesn't scream mafia, though. Hey, good luck with things on your end. I'll keep you posted if we come across anything else."

Peter disconnected the call, turned to his computer and typed 'Russian mafia.' Gleaning information from several sites, Peter found his lead. The Russian mafia committed typical crimes you would expect, but one of their chief rackets was buying real estate and businesses as a way to launder money acquired from their other illegal activities.

Travis stuck his head in the doorway.

"Hey, Boss. Missoula just called and said the rabies test on that dog was negative. Should I call Angus, or do you want to talk to him?"

"Go ahead and call him. If he asks, he's still on leave for two months."

Travis gave Peter a thumbs up and picked up the telephone handset from his desk.

Peter thought. *The Russian mafia has plenty of money and the ability to transfer an untraceable chunk to Bob's bank account. Bob owns a stretch of prime real estate along the highway, and someone has already drawn up plans to build a huge resort.*

He whistled to Zack, told Travis he was going out, then noticed the empty chairs and lack of a donut box.

"Where is everyone this morning?"

"Seems empty without Angus, doesn't it? Helen is probably still in bed and Tom is chasing cows off the road."

"Okay. Call me if you need me."

<hr>

PAUL ANSWERED THE door. "Hey, bro. What's going on?"

"I feel the need for cookies and conversation."

"Linda's in her study brainstorming a new book. Come on in. LINDAAAAAAAA," he hollered toward the back of the house.

Linda entered the kitchen as Paul arranged freshly baked snickerdoodles onto plates and Peter poured steaming hot water into his mug and coffee into theirs.

"Earl Grey?" asked Peter.

"In the cupboard," said Linda "What's new in the world of murder?"

Peter filled them in on the Russian mafia angle.

"So, the Russian mafia discovers Anderson and decides it will be a great place for a money laundering resort," said Linda. "They look at land records and find out Bob owns the land they want, see him for a stooge, and pay him a piddly amount of cash for his land. All's good until Bob tries to transfer ownership and can't because of the family covenants."

"He decides David is the key to getting past the covenants and starts calling to get him involved, but Dave doesn't have the power to change things and, not being a fan of Bob or his 'get rich quick' schemes, ignores him," continued Peter.

"The mafia had access to the land records. They may have been trying to get David's land, too. David won't deal with them, so they decide to eliminate him," said Paul.

"Or Bob did," offered Peter.

"Do you think Bob even knew he was dealing with the mafia?" asked Linda. "They probably passed themselves off as legitimate developers. How often does the mafia come and say, 'Hey, we're from the Russian mafia and we want to build a resort in your town'?"

"Good point," said Peter. "And I don't think Bob is dead. These guys don't have any qualms about killing and leaving the bodies. I think Bob walked in on the Sam killing and ran for his life."

"The question is how," said Linda. "He left his car in the parking lot and Zack lost his trail outside the bakery, so he must have escaped in another car. Did Bob have an accomplice?"

"Don't forget, Bob is still a suspect in Sam's murder. Sam was going to cut him off and ruin his business," said Peter.

"True. There are also the threatening letters to Sam and the poisoned pie for David. And why didn't the mafia go after Barb?" asked Paul. "It's not like she was under police protection. We didn't even know she'd left town."

"Barb doesn't have any claim over the property. She's insignificant. They think Bob is dead. They know Dave is dead . . . oh, no . . . they'll be going after the next person in line. Next after Bob is his son in Missoula and next after David is Holly!"

Peter was already out the door. He had to make sure Holly was safe.

Holly was at The Sapphire Pit working on account books. With Matthew on full time, she could skip the everyday bus ride up the mountain. She left a message at the sheriff's office for Peter about going into David's house and was waiting for a callback when Peter came running into the shop.

"We need to get out of here now!" shouted Peter

Holly looked at him as if he'd lost his mind. "What?!"

"Now, Holly. I'll explain on the way." He grabbed her arm and started pulling her toward the door.

Holly pulled back. "At least let me lock up the safe."

She gathered her ledgers and cash box, stacked them neatly on a shelf in the large wall safe, closed the door, and set the lock. Turning back to Peter, she saw the frightened look on his face. Peter wasn't afraid of anything . . . well, almost anything. Something had him spooked.

"Okay. Let's go," said Peter, propelling her through the shop, out the door, and into his still-running Explorer, parked just outside.

He ran around the vehicle and threw himself into his seat. "Buckle up!" he yelled as he slammed into gear and raced down the street.

"Peter! Slow down. You're going to hit someone. What's going on?"

Peter took a deep breath. He had Holly and she was safe for now.

"Bob and Dave were targeted by the Russian mafia. They want the land along the highway to build a resort. If they mistook Sam for Bob, they think Bob and Dave are both dead and will go after the heirs . . . that's you and Bob's son."

Holly stared at him, open-mouthed. "You're kidding. The Russian mafia? Have you been drinking?"

"I know it sounds crazy." He filled her in on the poisoned thug at the truck stop and his link to the Russian mafia.

"Where does this goofy poisoned pie thing fit in? The thug wouldn't have eaten it if he knew it was poisoned."

"Not a clue. My new favorite phrase," said Peter. He turned and gave her a wry smile.

"If the covenants say the land can't be developed, how can killing people change the outcome?" asked Holly.

"These people don't take 'no' for an answer. Maybe they didn't think a hundred-year-old land covenant would still hold. Which reminds me, I need to call the police chief in Missoula so he can get Bob's family into protection." He used his Bluetooth to request the call.

"Oh, no, Peter. Sally is an heir."

"Yep."

Peter gave the police chief the rundown and referred him to Sheriff Patterson if he had any questions. Then he called Nick Patterson.

"Hi, Peter. Anything new on your end of things?"

Peter explained his theory on the land deal. "I have one of the heirs with me and alerted the Missoula police chief. He's agreed to keep the Missoula family heirs in protective custody. Anyone come to claim Feliks's body?"

"We haven't been able to find or notify next of kin. The good news is the mafia doesn't know he's dead yet. It will buy us time."

"That's a relief," said Peter.

"He had a cellphone, but it's well encrypted. Our tech team is working on it."

"Thanks, Nick. Keep me posted."

"Welcome. Oh yeah, there's something else. We found a bag of uncut sapphires in his vehicle . . . guessing they came from Anderson."

"So, he was robbed," said Holly. "Angus was right."

Peter finished the call. "What do you mean 'Angus was right'?"

Holly sighed. "Angus wanted me to ask you if we could go into Uncle Dave's house and check his gem room. He thinks that Jensen woman tried to steal the sapphire. It sounds kind of silly now, but we drank quite a bit of beer before that."

"He needs a hobby," said Peter. "It's going to be a long two months."

"Can I tell him that the mafia stole the sapphires?"

"Sure, but remind him he's on leave for two months . . . that reminds me. We have to go to the house anyway and look for a roll of paper towels that will confirm the pie eaten by Feliks the thug came from David's house."

He turned the Explorer back up the hill towards David's house, watching for a tail.

"Bingo!" said Peter, picking up a roll of paper towels off the kitchen counter, still smeared with purple pie filling. He slipped the roll into an evidence bag and initialed the seal.

Holly was in the gem room. "Things have definitely been rifled through in here."

Peter poked his head in the door. Holly stood in front of a large storage cabinet full of small individual drawers. She turned to Peter, shocked.

"He had his sapphires weighed and classified in these drawers," said Holly. "They're all empty."

"Would David have emptied the drawers? Maybe he sold them to raise money?"

"I was in here last week and every drawer was full. Uncle David said nothing about getting rid of his stock."

"Either Feliks the thug had a side gig pawning stolen goods or someone else came in and cleaned those out. Meanwhile, we need to find a safe house for you until this thing gets straightened out."

"What about The Sapphire Pit? I do have a business to run."

"Can't your friend Matthew watch it for a while? He's all but a partner now."

"Yeah, I guess," Holly reluctantly conceded.

"My cabin has a full propane tank and fully-stocked pantry. Are you up to a hike?"

"Sure!" said Holly "I would love that. It would be like a vacation."

"We'll go by your house and get your hiking gear and anything else you want to bring along. You can stay with me tonight. I don't want to have to worry about the Russians coming by your place."

"What about my dad?"

"He can stay at my place too if he wants. Between the three of us we should be able to fend off a few Russians."

John surprised them both by agreeing to stay with them at Peter's house. "I'll go to the cabin with Holly, too. I don't plan on sitting around worrying about her."

Clothes, toiletries, and firearms loaded into back packs, the trio settled in at Peter's house.

"We'll leave at first light," John said. "Less chance of anyone noticing."

Knowing Holly and John were well armed and able to take care of themselves, Peter left to finish paperwork at the office. After he left, Holly's phone binged. Angus's name popped up.

"Hi, Angus. How are you feeling?"

"Good. I have an appointment with Dr. Hamm tomorrow. He's going to check everything out to make sure I'm healing okay. Hopefully, he can cast my arm."

"That sounds great! Hey, guess what. Peter and I went into the house today. Uncle Dave's gem room was ransacked. All the sapphires are gone."

"Any idea who did it?"

"The Russians probably."

Angus laughed. "The Russians?!"

"It's a long story, but . . . well, a Russian guy was found dead at the truck stop outside Clinton. He had a bag of uncut sapphires and he died from the same poison as Uncle David."

"No kidding?! Hey, why don't you come over tonight and tell me about it. We could order out again. The brewery has great pizza."

"I wish I could, Angus. Dad and I have to go into hiding. The Russians are looking for us. I'll tell you all about it when everything is over."

"Sure," said Angus, feeling out of the loop on the investigation. *Holly knows more about what's going on than I do,* he thought.

PETER FOUND TOM, Helen, and Travis gathered around a heaping plate of cookies. Mouth full and a cookie in each hand, Helen nodded hello. Travis had crumbs cascading down his shirt front.

"Linda thought we all needed a treat with this crazy Russian mob murder stuff going on," said Tom through a mouthful of cookie.

Sheesh, thought Peter. *It's like snack time at the grade school.*

"Nick Patterson called for you earlier," said Travis. "Do you want me to get him on the line?"

"Sure, thanks. I'll take it in my office."

A few moments later, Peter's office line beeped. "Hi, Nick. What's new?"

"This gets more and more interesting. Our tech guys got into Feliks's phone. Not many calls. We think he probably used a throwaway for a couple of days, then destroyed it and bought another one. But . . . one of the numbers that came up is registered to a Mrs. Olga Jensen, same address of the Olga Jensen who attacked your deputy."

"No kidding. Obnoxious soccer mom is in cahoots with the Russians?"

"Our savvy tech guys also looked into her background. Apparently, she's Feliks the thug's sister. We don't know how much she had to do with your sapphire guy's murder, but Feliks's texts to her confirm he performed the hanging. She was definitely aware of what was going on. She told her brother to make sure he got the 'stones' before he left the house."

"He was on his way to Missoula to give her the bag of sapphires."

"Yep. Good news is she won't be getting out of jail anytime soon. If they were far enough up in the chain of command, the Russians would have sprung her by now."

"Is the Missoula police department in the loop on this?"

"I talked to them before I called you. She's not talking and lawyered up. A public defender."

"Thanks for the update, Nick."

Peter disconnected, thought for a moment, then punched in the number for the Missoula police chief. After clearing things with Missoula, he joined his crew around the dwindling plate of cookies and updated them on the murders.

"First," started Peter, "is there anything going on around here that I need to know about?"

"A group of kids broke into the bakery last night and had a party," said Helen "After too many beers, one of them turned the lights on and I happened to be driving past. I cited them for MIP and trespassing. They were released to their parents."

"Jeez. I'm sure rumors of the gruesome murder have leaked out and they had to have a look. Hope they enjoy the nightmares," said Peter "We'd better keep a closer watch. There'll be more. Anything else?"

"Nope."

"Nothing important."

"Nada."

"Okay. Good. Helen, I want you to go to Missoula this afternoon and interview Bob Dahl's son and his wife, and Sally, too. They may have seen or heard things that would give us a clue to where Bob and Barb are hiding . . . if they are hiding. You might stress that they are in danger and in need of police protection."

"But if we're sure that Russian guy who died eating the poison pie is the killer, aren't they safe to come home?"

"No. That guy was just a hired thug for the mob. He was careless and got his sister involved. Whoever his bosses are still want ownership of Bob and David's property. They have no qualms about killing heirs standing in their way however pointless it is. Besides, Bob is still a murder suspect. He may have baked that pie and he may have pushed Sam into that mixer. We need to bring him in."

"What about Holly and her dad?" asked Travis.

"Already taken care of, but the fewer people who know the details, the better."

"Okay, Boss." Helen brushed the crumbs off her pants as she stood to leave.

Peter's phone pinged. Holly was calling. "Peter," said Holly, "we're getting nervous. My neighbor called and said there's a black Escalade circling the block."

"Okay. Sit tight and stay away from the windows. You need to get out of town sooner than planned."

He disconnected the call and ran out the door calling to Helen. She stopped at the foot of the stairs and turned around.

"Yeah, Boss?"

"I don't know if the Russians are aware of Bob's family in Missoula, but it looks like they might be back here staking out Holly's house. I'll call ahead and let Missoula know you need assistance after all. Be safe and watch your back."

"Sure, Boss," replied Helen, looking nervous.

Peter ran back up the stairs. "Tom, I need you to change into plain clothes and keep an eye on Holly's house. A black Escalade was reported to be circling the block. Use your own car. Follow carefully if necessary."

"Boss?"

"Yeah."

"What about Angus?"

"What about him?"

"I know he's on leave, but we're short of man-power. Holly lives across the street from the city park. Angus could sit there with his splinted arm and leg up on the park bench feeding pigeons and no one would be the wiser. He can keep me posted to Escalade sightings, and he'd be less likely to be spotted. Besides, it'll give him something to do. He's probably going stir crazy."

"Do we have pigeons in Anderson?"

Tom rolled his eyes. "You know what I mean."

"Okay. Change clothes and find Angus. Use your own judgement. If he's not up to it, don't even bring it up. And Tom . . ."

"Yeah, Boss?"

"These guys are ruthless and have no respect for small-town law enforcement. Take the tactical 870 and load it with lethals. Get a vest on, but don't try to take them on by yourself."

Tom gave Peter a thumbs up and headed into the break room to change. He always kept a spare set of clothes in the office, for just such an occasion.

Peter called Montana Highway Patrol and gave them a heads up to be nearby in case things escalated, and then drove home. So far, his house wasn't under surveillance. He needed to get Holly and John out of there and up to the cabin as soon as possible.

"We need to disguise you somehow," said Peter, as Holly looked doubtfully at the oversized men's jeans, long-sleeved plaid shirt, and baseball cap he held out for her. "Put these on and we'll stuff a pillow around the middle for a gut. Stuff your hair under the cap."

"Nobody's going to believe a chubby guy is hiking up the mountain."

"We add a fishing rod and tackle box and even the locals will think you're headed over to fish in the creek. By the time you get past there, you're in the trees and nobody can see you anyway.

"How are we going to disguise Dad?"

"Same thing. Add some padding, a baseball cap and a fishing rod. When have you ever seen your dad in anything but a cowboy hat?" said Peter, grinning at John. "I think he sleeps in the thing."

"I think it's grown to my head," joked John, belying the worry in his face.

"You can leave by my back door. Take the alleys as far as you can and avoid being seen."

Holly and John donned their disguises and emptied their backpacks, stowing as much as they could in the tackle boxes and underneath the oversized clothing. Backpacks would look too suspicious. Peter gave Holly a hug and shook John's hand.

"Be safe and stay put until I come to get you."

⸻⸻⸻

THE SLIGHT BREEZE down on the street turned to a brisk wind at the height of the bell tower where the watcher stood and, out of habit, calculated the shot as he observed two poorly-disguised 'fishermen' leave

Peter's house and make their way up the mountain. These animals were not natural prey and did not have the learned skills or inbred instincts to protect themselves. It was of no concern for the watcher. He needed his prey alive.

•••••••••

THE WINDOWS WERE open in Angus's apartment and Tom could hear faint music drifting out, even over the chatter of brewery patrons. He climbed the stairs and knocked on the door.

"Come in, it's open," yelled Angus

Angus sat in an easy chair, a paperback book in his hand, and a tall glass of beer on the table next to his chair.

"Getting used to the easy life?" asked Tom.

"I am," said Angus with a smile. "My sister Char brought over a box of books. I tried a Western, but I like the crime novels the best."

"How are you feeling?"

"Great. The swelling and pain are going down in both my arm and leg. I stopped taking those pain-killers and just use over-the-counter stuff when they start to ache. I have an appointment with Dr. Hamm tomorrow. If he casts my arm, I won't have to be quite so careful with it."

"Are you up to an undercover assignment?"

Angus's eyes lit up. "Boy, am I! What's going on?"

"Are you up to speed on the Russian issue?"

"Yeah, I talked to Holly this morning."

"One of David's neighbors reported seeing a black Escalade around David's house at the time of his murder. Now a neighbor of Holly's told her a black Escalade is circling the block about every half hour. We have to assume it's more Russians. Holly and her dad are safe, but we need to keep an eye on these guys. You with your arm sling and bum leg, sitting in the park reading your book won't look suspicious. I have a lawn chair in my trunk you can set out under the trees."

Angus pushed the footrest down on his recliner with his good leg and pushed himself up with his good arm. He hobbled over to a hall closet, pulled out a backpack and started loading it with beer and books.

"Put a ball cap on that red hair of yours," said Tom. "If the Russians have been hanging around for a while, they might recognize you. A pair of sunglasses wouldn't be out of line either."

"Sounds good," said Angus, so excited about getting out of his apartment that he didn't mind being teased about his hair.

Tom held onto Angus's arm while he hopped down the steep steps on one leg. He stowed the pack in the back seat, helped Angus into the passenger seat, and drove to the park. The two men parked, watched, and waited for the black Escalade to drive by. They weren't disappointed. Ten minutes into the wait, it slowly eased past, the man driving concentrating on Holly's house and not cars parked along the street.

"Let's go!" urged Tom, wanting to have Angus set up before the Escalade came back and saw his car. He pulled Angus's pack out of the back seat and the lawn chair from the trunk. After things were set up, he helped Angus hop over and settle in.

"Keep me posted. I'm going to be parked a couple blocks over so I can tail him when I get your call. I'll pick you up later," said Tom. "Consider this guy armed and dangerous," he warned.

"Got it," said Angus.

Angus lifted his face to the sun, felt the caress of a gentle breeze on his skin, and breathed in the scent of honeysuckle and freshly mown grass. All his life he'd been unaware of the beauty around him. What was it that his grandmother used to say? *"Slow down, Angus. You race so fast chasing life, you run right past it."*

14

ELEN OPENED THE door and settled herself into the passenger seat of the MPD undercover vehicle where Officer Glenn Hansen sat waiting. Already familiar with the case, Glenn was assigned to assist in any way necessary.

"No answer to the doorbell or knocking. Looks deserted," she said. "I walked around back. Nobody in the yard or on the deck. Two-car garage with one slot empty."

Helen's phone pinged. Peter.

"Hey, Boss."

"Just a heads up. The Russians are back in Anderson and watching Holly's house. They're most likely in Missoula. Keep your head on a swivel."

"Will do. Thanks."

While they waited, Helen gave Glenn a rundown of the Russian mafia situation. He was dumbfounded.

"Who would've thought we would be fighting the Russian mafia in Missoula, Montana."

He looked at his watch. "Do we know if they're even in town?"

"The Russians are driving by the house in Anderson about every half hour. We should wait at least that long and make sure they're not watching this house, too."

"What are the names of these people? I can run a license check. We can at least see if any of the vehicles on the street belong to them while we wait."

"Robert Dahl, Jr. and his wife Anne Marie. They have a daughter, Sally, age eighteen, newly graduated from Hellgate High School. Robert is an accountant. CPA. He works out of the house. Anne Marie is a homemaker."

Glenn ran the check, waited while the results came through, and looked around. Just then a green Subaru Forrester drove past and pulled into the Dahl's driveway. As the doors on the car opened and a middle-aged couple climbed out, a black Escalade, tires squealing, came around the corner, the black barrel of a gun poking out the window.

Helen stuck her head out and yelled, "Get down!!!"

The couple turned to look toward her but obeyed and dropped down to the cement driveway as shots rang out. Glenn turned on his siren and lights. The passenger in the Escalade continued to shoot toward the Subaru while the driver hit the gas and sped away. Glenn paused briefly to let Helen out, then picked up his mic to call for backup and began pursuit.

Helen ran to the Subaru. Out of breath from exertion and the adrenaline rush, she dropped down next to the car. When she confirmed both people were unharmed, she introduced herself.

"Robert and Anne Marie Dahl?" she asked.

The couple nodded in unison, still too shocked to speak

"Let's go inside and I'll explain everything," said Helen as she stood and helped the couple to their feet.

A sidewalk leading to the rambling rancher-style house split halfway along, the right branch marked by a decorative wooden sign announcing 'Dahl House Accounting' veered off and wound around to a separate side entrance. The left branch continued straight, leading to an old-fashioned veranda, complete with rocking chairs and a porch swing. Robert led the way to the main entrance, glancing nervously down the street as he unlocked the door.

The Dahls were understandably shook up. Helen sat them in the living room, found her way to the kitchen and proceeded to make tea. When the three of them were settled, Helen gave them a brief rundown of everything that had occurred since the probable attempt on Bob Dahl's life.

"Do you know why your dad would get involved with the Russian mafia or take money from them?" asked Helen.

Robert sighed. "Dad is a hard worker and has a great business there in Anderson. He makes a good profit, but he has a heart of gold and no common sense when it comes to money. He doesn't invest to keep his own equipment up to date but will give thousands of dollars to other people. Last year he wrote a check for ten thousand dollars to a bakery in Nimrod, a competitor, because he heard their refrigerator was broken. His own refrigerator was running on duct tape and paperclips. A few years ago, he bought uniforms for the little league teams, not just in Anderson, but the neighboring towns, too. When the inspectors told him his equipment wasn't safe and needed to be replaced, he had no savings and no credit at the bank. He told me he found 'business investors' to loan him money. I thought it sounded suspicious. I never imagined his investors were the mafia."

"What about your mom? Did she have a say in any of this?"

"Mom wasn't interested in the business. She was happy to sit home and do her quilting and gardening and take care of all those feral cats. In her mind, as long as she had a working credit card, all was good."

"As an accountant, did you handle your dad's books?"

"I tried. I offered to do them for free, but Dad didn't want me to have anything to do with them. I don't think he wanted me to know how bad things were, especially when he started borrowing money from thugs."

"Which brings us to the next issue. We need to get you out of here and into protective custody."

"I guess I don't understand why they're after us."

"They probably think you can lead them to your father, and they want that land. Where's Sally?"

"She has a job at the Southgate Mall in the food court," said Anne Marie "Where are we going to go?"

"There are safe houses. We'll bring Sally there, too."

Helen called into the MPD and explained the situation.

"We'll send an officer. He'll be able to transport the family to a safe house."

Helen verified the name and badge number of the responding officer and disconnected. She instructed the couple to pack one small suitcase each with changes of comfortable clothing and any personal items they would need for several days.

"Food, basic toiletries, and laundry facilities will be available at the safe house," said Helen.

"Do you know the whereabouts of your parents?" she asked, as the couple packed.

"I have no idea. We haven't heard from them," said Robert.

"We're mostly concerned with their safety and want to verify they are alive. Also, your father may have witnessed the murder of Sam Geary in the bakery."

"We don't know where they are or where they might be hiding. We've been racking our brains trying to figure it out," said Anne Marie. "Sally's busy with registering for college and working at the food court. We haven't had much chance to talk with her either."

"She must have been close to her grandparents. Did she seem upset about their disappearance?"

"Not really." She glanced at her husband, a silent message passing between them.

"Sally lives in her own world," said Robert. "She's sweet and kind and is either oblivious to the evils of the world or chooses to block them out."

The apple doesn't fall far from the tree, thought Helen, wondering about a man who would name his professional business 'Dahl House.'

"I need to interview Sally," said Helen. "Many times, people know facts they don't realize are important."

The doorbell chimed. Helen motioned for the Dahls to stay put and fingered the window curtain open just enough to see an MPD cruiser at the curb. She walked to the door and peeked through the peep hole. The officer held his badge and stood so his nameplate was easily seen and read. Helen opened the door.

"Officer Wilson, ma'am. I'm here for a safe house transfer."

Helen motioned to Robert and Anne Marie and held the door while they shuffled through with their bags. When the group came to the street, Wilson motioned to a slim athletic young woman in faded jeans and a long-sleeved plaid shirt waiting next to a Jeep Cherokee parked behind the MPD cruiser.

"Officer Harris will transport Mr. and Mrs. Dahl to their safe house and stay with them as long as protection is required," said Wilson.

Helen was reminded once again of her own lapsed fitness as she watched a strong and healthy Harris collect the suitcases and toss them into the back of the Cherokee with little effort. Even in plain clothes she easily passed for a police officer. *Would anyone mistake me for a police officer out of uniform?* thought Helen as she began to follow Robert and Anne Marie to the Cherokee.

"Wait," called Wilson. The three of them stopped and turned. "Mr. and Mrs. Dahl will be safe with Officer Harris. Ferguson, you and I will collect Sally Dahl from the Southgate Mall. We have another plain clothes officer who will transport her to the safe house when you're finished with your questioning."

Helen smiled encouragingly toward the Dahls. She hadn't known them long enough to feel any protective attachment. Settled in the cruiser for the long drive through the city, Helen thanked the officer for his help. She stopped herself from giving him a rundown of the situation. Less people in the inner circle meant less chance of a hole in the fence.

Sally recognized Helen as an Anderson sheriff deputy so followed her with little hesitation to the patrol car. Wilson stayed back and assured Sally's manager that she wasn't in any trouble but was needed as a witness in connection to a serious crime and would be absent from work for an indefinite period of time. He could almost see the wheels in the man's head spinning out scenarios.

Back in the car, Helen and Wilson sat in the front keeping close watch in rear and side view mirrors for any kind of tail.

"Where are you taking me?" asked Sally.

"To the Missoula police department first," said Wilson. "Officer Ferguson needs to ask you a few questions. It will be safe there."

"Afterwards," said Helen "A plain clothes officer will drive you to a safe house to be with your parents."

"Safe house?" exclaimed Sally. "Why am I going to a safe house? What is this all about?"

"Your parents are already on their way there," said Helen. "I'll tell you everything when we get to the station."

"Are my parents okay?"

"Yes, and we want to make sure you stay safe. Don't contact anyone, even a best friend. Turn off all tracking devices on your phone."

"Okay. You're really scaring me."

"Being scared will keep you safe. Stay vigilant."

Updated recently, the Missoula police department had several comfortable 'witness' rooms. Wilson led Helen and Sally to one of these rooms and instructed Helen to call him when they were ready for transport. Sally by this time was near tears from worry and confusion.

"Would you like something to drink? A cup of coffee or a pop?" asked Helen.

"A Pepsi would be nice."

Helen noticed a bank of drink and snack machines along the opposite wall when they entered the witness room. She loaded the Pepsi machine with slightly-wrinkled dollar bills and crossed her fingers it wouldn't spit them out while she punched the button for a Pepsi. Success. Helen stood staring at the machines, an internal war raging. She felt old, fat, and out of shape after recent events. Her stomach growled loudly. Finally, she settled for a Diet Pepsi and bought two bags of peanuts. At least it wasn't a candy bar.

Helen closed the door gently behind her as she re-entered the witness room. Sally, head in hands, was quietly sobbing. Helen tapped her gently on the shoulder and handed her the Pepsi and a bag of peanuts as Sally straightened and wiped tears from her face. The room was surprisingly comfortable, painted in a serene pale blue and furnished with comfortable padded chairs.

"This doesn't look like the interrogation rooms on TV," said Sally.

"That's because it isn't an interrogation room. You're not in any trouble, Sally. We're really worried about the safety of you and your parents and grand-parents."

"I don't understand what's going on. Why is someone trying to hurt my family?"

"We have reason to believe there are some very bad men who want control of your grandfather's property."

"The house? The bakery?"

"No, his other property."

"What other property?"

If there was any doubt about Sally being involved in the extortion, that rules that out, thought Helen.

"Long story. I'll let your parents tell you about that. Do you know where your grandfather got the money to remodel the bakery?"

"Some businessmen came to the bakery a few times. Grandpa was really excited about it. He made special pastries just for them."

"Can you tell me anything about them?"

"They were really nice. They always brought me a present." She pulled her hair back and showed Helen what looked like authentic diamond and sapphire earrings. "Aren't they beautiful?"

"Yes, they're very beautiful. Did these men ever ask you for favors?"

"No, they just talked to me. They were so nice. They had a funny accent so sometimes I couldn't understand them, and they would laugh and talk really slow."

Helen faked a laugh. "Did they tell you where they were from, why they had an accent?"

"They said they were from Europe."

"Just Europe? Nothing specific?"

"No."

"What else did you talk about?"

"They asked me about my job at the bakery and if I helped Grandpa with the books and stuff. They always said I was so smart I should be running the place." Sally smiled remembering.

"They sound wonderful. Anything else?"

"They asked about my parents and where I live and stuff."

"What did you tell them?"

"Well, you know, just about our house in Rattlesnake Canyon and how beautiful it is there and how Dad has his office in the house and how excited I was about graduating from Hellgate High this year."

"They never asked you about other land your grandpa owned?"

"They said something about it once, but I said Grandpa didn't own any other land."

Sally yawned and fidgeted, and Helen's stomach growled again. "Okay," she said. "Just one more thing. Do you have any idea where your grandparents are? Where they would go to hide out."

Sally stared at the wall for a moment, thinking. "Maybe the lake."

"The lake? What lake?"

"Yeah, Georgetown. I heard them talking about it a couple days before the murder and Grandpa went missing. They were arguing in the back office so they probably didn't know I could hear. I wasn't eavesdropping," she added, a flash of guilt passing over her face.

"I'm sure your grandparents would want you to help us help them in any way you can. Can you remember any specifics?"

"They said something about staying on a boat and their friends wouldn't be using it this summer because one of them is sick with cancer."

Bingo, thought Helen. "Thank you for all your help, Sally."

Helen took a business card out of a case in her pocket. "Remember, DON'T use your cell phone unless it's to call me or another officer."

Helen handed Sally over to a plain clothes officer, this time a middle-aged man with a paunch. Helen, relieved it wasn't another young and fit woman, felt a little bit better about herself.

15

While Tom and Angus staked out Holly's house, Matthew held down the fort at The Sapphire Pit. Thrilled with the opportunity to show Holly he could manage things while she was gone, he worked extra hard to make sure the paying guests had a good time and were likely to return. Holly's Uncle David was a loss, but Matthew was sure he could find another assistant to take his place. Matthew considered himself average in looks, average in build, and average in personality. He didn't have great wealth to offer Holly and knew she still held feelings for Anderson's handsome and popular sheriff, but Matthew had something Peter didn't have, he had the same passion for gems and The Sapphire Pit as Holly. Matthew would happily be a life partner to Holly in every way. He was lost in a daydream of their life together as husband and wife when a gruff accented voice startled him awake.

"Excuse me."

Matthew glanced up at the shadow blocking the sun and shivered, but from fear rather than cold. A menacing chill radiated from the two men standing in front of him. Dressed all in black: black loafers and black slacks, black long-sleeved button-down shirts cut to lie well so as to not require a tuck-in.

Hiding guns, thought Matthew, all too aware of the pistol in his own waistband.

"We're looking for Holly," said the taller one on the right.

"She's n . . . n . . . not here," said Matthew, a slight stammer betraying his nervousness.

"Where did she go?" asked the same man.

"I don't know," replied Matthew, calculating his odds in a gun fight against the thugs and doubting it would come out well for him.

"When will she be back?"

"I don't know."

"You expect me to believe she left you in charge of her business and you don't know where she went or when she would be back?

"She said it was personal. Her uncle just died. I assumed she was doing family stuff," said Matthew, now annoyed and defiant at the attitude of the thugs.

He caught his breath as the two men turned and walked away without another word. He dropped his head onto the table.

"Are you okay, mister?" asked a small voice.

Matthew raised his head. A girl with curly black hair stood in front of his table with a concerned look on her young face. He randomly wondered if that's what Holly looked like we she was a little girl.

"Yeah, I'm great," he croaked.

Matthew looked at his watch and was relieved to see it was a few minutes past official closing time. No need to be overly polite as he shooed out the last few stragglers.

When the final pail of dirt disappeared out the door, Matthew locked up and left without worrying about cleanup. He let himself out the back door, looking left and right down the alley before climbing into his Jeep Wrangler and driving straight to the sheriff's office. After Illegally parking in front of a fire hydrant, he took the marble steps into the courthouse two at a time. He ran straight past Travis at his desk and plopped, breathing hard, into the leather chair in front of Peter, for once thrilled to see his nemesis.

Peter looked up from his paperwork, surprised to see a panting Matthew at his desk.

"What's going on Matt?" he asked.

"Two guy . . . thugs . . . looking for Holly."

"Aahhhh," said Peter. "No worries. Holly and her dad are safe. I'm not going to tell you where. Safer for you not to know."

"But, why? What's going on?" asked Matthew.

"It's a long story. I'll let Holly tell you all about it when it's over. I don't think they'll bother you anymore," said Peter, hoping he was right. "You didn't notice anyone follow you here?"

"No, but I was so worried about Holly, I wasn't really paying attention. There wasn't anyone waiting outside The Pit when I left."

"Good. Just make sure your doors are locked and keep an eye out for strangers."

Peter gave Matthew his cell phone number. "Call me immediately if anything else happens. Anytime day or night," he added.

Hesitant, Matthew stood, turned, and walked into the outer office. Travis gave him a compassionate look. He knew how much Matthew cared for Holly and the frustration he must be feeling.

"She's safe, Matt," said Travis.

"Thanks, Travis."

After Matthew left, Peter called Tom. "The thugs were at The Sapphire Pit looking for Holly."

"Yeah, they drove by just now and I'm following them. They're headed out of town. Do you want me to continue pursuit?"

"Do you have visual on the license plate number?"

Tom relayed the number and description of the vehicle he was following.

"Thanks," said Peter. "Continue tailing, but don't engage. I'll relay this info to Missoula County, and they can pick up the tail when you reach the county line."

Peter relayed the info to the Missoula County sheriff's office and then ran a trace of the vehicle license plates. He fought back the urge to hike to his cabin. Any chance of someone watching him would put Holly and John in danger.

Tom tailed the black Escalade until a few miles beyond the Stone County line. The thugs were careful. He would have had a hard time coming up with a valid reason for pulling them over. A beat-up blue Ford pulled out of a ranch road and signaled to him. *Nice cover*, he thought. Tom slowed down at the next county road, turned, drove far enough to look legitimate, pulled a U-ey and headed back home.

⬥⬥⬥

AS MUCH AS he was enjoying his newfound appreciation of leisure time, Angus was bored after most of a day sitting in the same spot at the park. He was thrilled when Tom pulled up to the curb.

"Ready to pack it up?" asked Tom.

"Am I!" said Angus. "Drop me off at the brewery. I could use some conversation after sitting in the park all day. Bud will help me back up the stairs."

Tom dropped Angus off in front of the brewery. *Getting hurt may have been a blessing for Angus,* thought Tom. *He's never been so, well, happy.*

16

"WE REALLY NEED to hire a night-shift deputy," said Helen, tired from her day in Missoula and a busy night on call.

"The position is posted," sighed Peter. "Just waiting for a qualified candidate."

As popular as Anderson was as a leisure destination, few people actually wanted to move there for work and housing costs had risen out of reach for most middle to lower income people who didn't own homes before the housing crunch.

Helen eyed the donut box. Being overtired and hungry made it harder to resist. She decided she would limit herself to one but pick her favorite: chocolate-frosted Boston crème.

"How did things go yesterday in Missoula?" asked Peter.

Helen told him about the attack at the Dahl house and moving Robert, Anne Marie, and Sally to a safe house.

"Okay, good," said Peter. "More people safe."

"The other good news is Sally gave me a lead on a possible hiding place for Bob and Barb."

Everyone perked up with interest. Helen told them about the possibility of the Dahls hiding in a boat at Georgetown Lake.

"It would have to be some sort of houseboat," said Travis.

"Good thought," said Peter. "Can you get me a list of boat slips, renters, and boat types if possible. I'll go over this afternoon and check them out."

"Sure, Boss."

The meeting over, Peter went to his office and noticed the message-light blinking. He punched the button. After several calls about minor local incidents that he forwarded to Travis, the voice of the Missoula County sheriff came online, "Peter, we have more dead Russians. Call me."

Why not? thought Peter. He hit the call-back button and listened to the phone ring. Voicemail picked up and he started to leave a message when the call was picked up.

"Sheriff Patterson."

"Hi, Nick. This is Peter Elliot in Stone County returning your call."

"Peter! Good news. We caught your Russian mafia guys . . . at least the two who tried to take out Robert and Anne Marie Dahl."

"Caught as in recovered dead bodies?"

"Well, yeah. Police officer on the scene with your deputy at the Dahl house chased them up Pattee Canyon road. He's a local. Knows the road blindfolded. They missed a curve and went over the edge. We pulled the bodies out of the wreckage late last night."

"Identification?"

"No IDs like the last guy, but fingerprints came back hot. Petty thugs with a long list of priors."

"Any connection to the Russian mafia?"

"Nope. Vehicle registered to that same blanket corporation. AK-47s and 9mm Makarov pistols all with the serial numbers professionally removed, but we can at least prove they were the guns used in the shooting at the Dahl house."

"I wonder why the mob doesn't hide the identity of these guys better."

"They're throwaways. The mob doesn't care as long as they don't get traced back to the organization. These guys never talk because they know it's a death sentence."

"Noted. Thanks for the info, Nick. Keep me posted."

"Likewise, Peter. We'll catch these guys eventually."

Peter disconnected as Travis walked into his office.

"There are two private marinas at Georgetown Lake. I explained the situation and they were happy to help a police investigation. There are a total of seventy slips available, but only half of those are rented out for the season. Both marinas faxed over a list of long-term boat slip renters and the type of boat registered. I crossed out the boats that don't have living space. That leaves twenty-two boats that could be a hiding place for the Dahls. Do we know the name of their friends with the boat?"

"No," sighed Peter. "But twenty-two possibilities are better than no lead at all. I better get started," he said as he stood and grabbed his hat off the hook behind his desk. "Come on, Zack. Let's roll."

Trout Haven Marina sat a short thirteen miles from Anderson, as the crow flies. The twists and turns of a mountain pass added seven miles and an extra fifteen minutes of driving time. Peter pulled into the marina just short of half an hour after he left the courthouse. He parked by the marina office so he could introduce himself and let them know he was there. Peter whistled and held the door open so Zack could join him. A rusty-looking old sailor manned the till, most likely a lifetime fisherman earning his rights to a boat slip by filling in as little as possible.

"Have you noticed this couple living on any of the boats this summer?" asked Peter, showing the old man a picture of Barb and Bob.

"All kinds of people living on the boats. Not my job to keep track of everyone."

No help coming from him, thought Peter, but he thanked the man and gave him a card.

"Please give me a call if you should happen to think of anything that would help."

Glancing back on his way out the door, Peter saw the man drop his card behind the counter. *Straight into the garbage.* The man saw Peter watching and sneered maliciously. *The world is full of bitter nasty people. Glad I'm not you,* thought Peter. Zack eyed the man and growled as they walked out the door.

Trout Haven was the most popular and conveniently located of the two marinas so seventeen of the twenty-two livable boats were parked there. Peter looked at his list, trying to narrow his search. The people who owned the boat he was looking for were friends of Bob and Barb and the wife of the couple was fighting cancer, so Peter assumed they were of the same age as the Dahls and, therefore, did not have young children. Boat slip renters were not only listed by type of boat, but also number of people in residence. He put stars by the boats with only two people, presumably older couples, rather than families. That reduced the list to seven boats. The marina had two docks, one on each end of the property. They usually assigned boats with families to the dock closest to the water park, keeping the kids and noise together. Peter made his way to the far end of the property where retirees looking for peace and quiet dwelled. Slip numbers were painted in white on a post in front of each slip. Of the slips on Peter's list, four were pairs next to each other and were rented by couples with the same last name . . . brothers and their wives? Peter decided to check the remaining three first. Slip one held an older model Catalina 28 sailboat with a youngish-looking couple busy hauling boxes of supplies onto the boat from a nearby SUV.

"Hello," said Peter, showing his badge.

The couple looked surprised to see a sheriff on the dock but were curious and friendly.

"I'm looking for a couple in regard to an investigation. They're not suspects but may have information to help us with the case. We have reason to believe they are staying on a boat on the lake."

"What can we do to help?" asked the man.

Peter took a picture of Bob and Barb Dahl out of his pocket and showed it to the couple.

"I haven't seen anyone who looks like that," said the woman "Have you Rick?"

"No, but we just got here," said Rick.

Peter thanked them for their help and moved on to slip eleven.

An older couple of the right age range sat on the deck of a roomy apple-red trawler, sipping cocktails and watching as Peter approached. He stopped at the edge of the dock and held his hand, and badge, up in greeting.

"Howdy, Sheriff," said the man. "Come aboard."

Peter caught hold of the ladder and hoisted himself into the boat. Zack whined at the edge of the dock.

"Stay Zack. I'll be right back."

"We're having rum and cokes, but there is a full bar, including beer if you prefer."

"None for me, thanks. I'm on duty."

"A beer for the dog then? Or is he on duty too?"

Peter laughed. "Zack doesn't drink beer until after five."

"Aaahhhh. We respect a dog with principles."

"I hope we haven't done anything to get on the wrong side of the law," said the woman, giving Peter a flirtatious wink.

"Not that I'm aware of." He handed the picture of Bob and Barb to the wife, who studied it and then passed it on to her husband.

"I'm looking for this couple, in regard to an investigation. We have reason to believe they are docked on the lake somewhere. Have either of you seen them?"

"They aren't on this dock," said the man. "We've been here all season so we would have seen them."

The wife reached out to retrieve the picture and studied it for another minute.

"Hmmmm. I think I've seen this woman at the marina store. I remember her because she was being really rude to the clerk. She wanted something exotic, and he kept trying to explain that it was a convenience store and not a high-end supermarket."

"She didn't happen to say where she was staying?"

"No," laughed the woman. "But George is right. If they were on this dock, we would know. Have you tried the other marina?

"My next stop," said Peter as he turned to climb back down the ladder. "Thanks for your help. Enjoy your afternoon."

"Come back for that beer when you're off duty," said George.

Peter made his way back down the dock, Zack barely containing the urge to run around sniffing and exploring the new surroundings.

"When we're done," said Peter, "we'll find a place for you to run."

Zack looked up with a doggie grin, tail wagging.

Peter opened the door so Zack could jump into the back of his vehicle and then settled himself in the driver's seat. He studied the map he had picked up on the way out of the Trout Haven Marina office. Thankful for well-marked roads, Peter slowly bumped his way over ruts and puddles on the neglected dirt road leading to the far side of the lake where he found an aptly named Pine Haven Marina nestled in a hollow of pine trees between the Pintler Mountains and Georgetown Lake. The marina office was a self-pay kiosk built at the entrance of a dead-end road. Ignoring faded red letters stenciled on the side of the kiosk demanding payment of a day use fee for every vehicle entering the marina, Peter followed the road to a clearing outlined by a scattering of camping sites and anchored at the far end by a large pavilion filled with sagging picnic tables and a crumbling brick grill. Pine Haven Marina was no doubt the low-rent district of the lake. Everything, including the few inhabitants, had an air of decay and seediness. Peter parked, safety checked his weapon and called into the office to notify Travis of his location. He felt watching eyes as he rolled up the windows, exited the vehicle and opened the rear door for Zack. He made a show of locking and double checking the doors before he walked over to the small twelve slip dock making up the whole of the marina. Records showed five livable boats at the marina, but there were only four docked. None of them looked seaworthy, let alone livable. The cove sheltering the marina was too small and the water too murky to attract a more affluent clientele. As

Peter stood on the dock, scanning his surroundings for signs of life, Zack let out a low growl and fixed his eyes on the deck of a rusty trawler. On board, sitting on an old whiskey barrel was a man as grimy as his boat. Without the warning from Zack, he would have continued to blend into the colors of the trawler and Peter would have walked past unaware.

"Come aboard if you must, Sheriff," said the crusty old sailor. "I ain't had the gumption to scorn the law for a long time gone so I know you're not lookin' for me."

Peter climbed aboard, leaving Zack to stand watch. He saw an amber bottle in the sailor's hand and was surprised to see it was a bottle of root beer rather than its alcohol-filled cousin.

"Hankerin' for a cold one?" asked the sailor, not waiting for an answer, but reaching down to his side and pulling another bottle of root beer out of a battered Igloo cooler.

Peter took the bottle with his left hand and offered his right for a handshake.

"Peter Elliott, Stone County sheriff."

"Preston Clairmont," said the sailor with a grip of rare strength for a man his age. "My dear mother had higher hopes for me than I had an inclination to achieve. My friends and enemies call me Stony to my face."

"And I will call you Stony to your face and otherwise. Very pleased to make your acquaintance."

"Now that we've covered the formalities, Peter, you seem to be on the wrong side of your county line. What brings you to this lonely lagoon?"

Peter took the picture of Barb and Bob out of his front shirt pocket and handed it to Stony. "I'm looking for this couple in regard to an investigation. We have reason to believe they are staying on a boat on this lake."

"Yep. They've been here for a bit. Goin' on half hour ago, they got all in a fuss, pulled anchor and left."

"What sort of boat?"

"A rusty old tub of the same ilk as this one I call home. I wouldn't have bet a plug nickel that thing would run, but it's the same one that brought them here."

"Can you tell me anything else that might help? Anything they may have said while they were here?"

"Nah. They warn't a bit friendly. I thought they acted fair high an' mighty considering their location and livin' quarters."

Stony winced as he stood, with the stiffness brought on by arthritis and too long sitting on a whiskey barrel stool. He walked into his cabin and, after rummaging through a drawer, brought out a slip of paper and a photograph that he handed to Peter.

"I had a hunch those two were up to no good. Here's the HIN number for their boat. I shot that picture through my cabin window last week when they warn't payin' attention and had it developed at the pharmacy in Rumsey."

Peter looked at the picture. A couple stood rigidly on the deck of a rusty decrepit trawler, not unlike the one where Peter was sitting. Bob and Barb Dahl stared toward shore with the same expression Peter had seen on every criminal he was about to arrest, the face of a trapped animal.

"They got real antsy every time a new vehicle pulled into the parking lot," said Stony.

Peter stood to leave. "I need to find them before they disappear again. Do you have any idea which direction they may be heading?"

"There's only one place on the lake that allows long term overnight parking. That's the Moose Meadows boat launch. Folks can park there and boat to campgrounds across the lake that aren't reachable by car. That old boat was headed in that general direction."

"Thanks, Stony. You've been a great help. If you ever need anything . . ."

"Come back 'n tell me how this all works out." He lifted his bottle. "And bring a fresh six-pack."

"Will do."

Peter climbed off the boat and hurried to his vehicle, Zack close at his heels. Knowing he couldn't beat the Dahl's boat around the lake to Moose Meadows, he radioed into the office.

"Travis, I need you to send whoever is available immediately to a Moose Meadows boat launch at Georgetown Lake. I have reason to believe Bob and Barb Dahl are on their way there in a rusty old trawler. Barb's car is probably parked there; she drives an orange Nissan Rogue, and whatever Bob was driving when he disappeared. I'm on the other side of the lake. Detain them until I get there."

"Got it, Boss. Helen and Tom are on their way."

"Roger."

Peter drove as fast as he could down the choppy road, banging his head and other assorted body parts multiple times against the inside of the Explorer. Zack eventually gave up and crouched on the floor between the seats.

He stopped for a moment at a crossroads and studied his map. Moose Meadows was just off the main highway at the far end of the lake.

When Peter pulled into the upper lot, reserved for long-term parking, he spotted Tom and Helen standing next to Barb's garish orange Rogue, but no sign of Bob and Barb. *Shoot! They got away,* he thought.

He rolled down his window. "No sign of them?" he asked.

Tom and Helen both pointed toward Helen's patrol car.

"Cuffed and Mirandaed," said Helen.

Tom was holding a wad of bloody Kleenex around his nose. He had three parallel scratches down the side of his face. His eyes were swollen and red.

"What happened?" asked Peter.

"They saw us waiting for them when they came up the hill from the boat ramp and made a run for it. Tom caught up to Barb first and she attacked him. She whacked him in the nose with her purse and scratched him when he tried to cuff her. Bob got in the middle of it and started pummeling him with anything he could find."

"Yikes!!! How did you get them both cuffed and in the car?"

"Pepper spray," said Helen, looking slightly sheepish. "Unfortunately, Tom got the worst of that, too."

"Did you get anything out of Bob and Barb?"

"No. They lawyered up pretty fast, but at least we have them for resisting arrest and assaulting a police officer."

Peter looked around and noticed Tom's patrol vehicle parked next to Helen's, and next to that a classic fire-engine red 1966 Galaxy 500 Special Addition, two-door hard top.

"Wow!" he said. "Whose car is that?"

"Bob's," said Helen. "We forgot about it when we were trying to figure out how he left Anderson. Remember when he used to drive it in the town parades every year?"

"Oh, yeah," said Peter. "I wonder where he kept it."

"Tom said he used to store it in that old garage in back, but Barb's cats kept crawling under the cover and scratching it up. He moved it to a garage he had in the alley next to the bakery."

"Barb failed to mention that," said Peter. He looked back, seeing a miserable Tom.

"Tom, you ride back with me, and we'll stop over at the hospital and get you checked out. We can come back for your rig later."

Tom nodded and felt his way along the hood of the Explorer with one hand, holding his nose with the other, until Helen took pity on him and led him to the door.

After Tom was buckled in, Peter said, "Helen, I'll radio ahead and have Travis meet you outside. I don't want you trying to get those two inside by yourself."

Helen nodded in acknowledgement and walked back to her car.

Peter turned to Tom. "Is it still bleeding?"

Tom pulled the blood-saturated wad of Kleenex away from his nose.

"Can't see."

Crusty patches of dried blood dotted Tom's face and upper lip, but any flow of fresh blood was gone.

"You're good," Peter said as he dug through the console and pulled out a bottle of saline eye drops. "Here, rinse your eyes with these."

Tom tossed the bloody wad on the seat and fumbled with the bottle of eye drops until he managed to get several drops in each eye. "Aaaaaahhhh! That stings," he said as he started to rub his eyes.

"Stop!" yelled Peter, grabbing Tom's arm. "Don't rub them. It'll just make it worse, and you might have pepper spray on your hands."

"And I thought Black Friday sales at the grocery store were dangerous," said Tom.

Peter silently prayed Tom wouldn't hang up his badge. He couldn't afford to lose another deputy.

So much for 'You have the right to remain silent,' thought Helen as she listened to Barb and Bob screaming at each other in the back of the car.

Barb: "I should have listened to my parents. They told me you were a loser on day one."

Bob: "I've worked my butt off supporting you for thirty years while you sat on yours watching soaps and eating too many bonbons. Look at your butt in the mirror if you don't believe me."

Barb: "I gave birth to your two children and raised them. That's not nothing. What kind of idiot makes business deals with the mafia?!"

And on and on it went. Helen would have turned on the radio to drown them out if she hadn't been more worried about missing something important to the case.

"Did you get anything more out of them?" asked Peter.

Helen, Peter, and Travis were sitting in the outer office eating stale donuts left over from the day before and comparing notes after the Dahls were booked into the county jail. Tom was released from Stone County Medical Center and sent home for the rest of the day.

"No. They argued all the way home, but nothing we don't already know."

"They're running from more than the mafia," said Peter. "Any guesses what they're hiding?"

"Not a clue."

17

"I've got a hit, Peter," said Travis.

Peter forced his eyes open to look at the bedside clock.

"Travis. It's five-thirty in the morning. Why aren't you in bed? Sleeping. Like sane people."

"That third set of fingerprints on the Sam Geary letters was bugging me. They looked familiar, but I couldn't think of why. I couldn't sleep so I came into the office."

"Some people drink a glass of warm milk."

"I took all the fingerprints we've fumed since the beginning of these murders . . . everything from the bakery and David's house . . . and compared them to the prints on those letters."

"What did you find?"

"Nothing at first. I thought it was just wishful thinking. Then I compared them to the prints on the business card. They matched. I double-checked with the fingerprint cards we collected from Clay and the Gearys. Clay is a perfect match for the prints on the letters."

"Would there be any reasonable explanation for Clay's prints to be on the Geary letters?"

"Not unless he wrote or delivered them. Didn't Seth tell you nobody touched them except he and Sam?"

"Yes, he did," said Peter, already out of bed and pulling on his blue jeans. "Good work, Travis. Is Helen anywhere close? I'm going to need backup."

"Already here waiting."

Peter drove to the courthouse and found Helen waiting out front holding a white take-out bag from Dixie's Diner.

"I had Dixie pack us a couple of breakfast sandwiches."

Peter's stomach growled. Dixie made world-class breakfast sandwiches. Eggs, bacon, sausage, and some kind of secret sauce beyond compare.

"Thanks, Helen. I never think to eat until I'm on the road."

"I know," said Helen, mouth full of sandwich. "Are we going to arrest Clay on the spot or bring him in for questioning?"

"Both, unless he can give us a reasonable explanation why his prints are on those letters."

By the time Peter pulled up to the old ranch house, the sun was peeking through Gunsight Ridge and the breakfast bag was empty. A lifetime of rising with the sun had Clay already out warming up his tractor. He pushed away from the open engine compartment and wiped his hands on a greasy rag, an air of resignation in his stance.

"Sheriff. Deputy. What brings you here so early in the morning?"

Helen unclipped a pair of handcuffs from her belt and proceeded to inform Clay of his right to remain silent as she drew his hands behind him and fastened them into the cuffs.

"What got you onto me?"

"Fingerprints on the letters."

"Careless of me."

"You can tell us about it back in town," said Peter as he led Clay to the back seat of the Tahoe.

"Hey, Sheriff."

"Yeah, Clay."

"Could you turn off my tractor? I'd hate to waste all that gas."

Later, in the sheriff's office, Clay waived his right to an attorney.

"Yeah, I put those letters in Sam's delivery truck, but I didn't write them," said Clay, face down in shame.

"Who did write them?" asked Peter.

"That snake Winston Hayes. He mailed them to me in bigger envelopes and then I put them in Sam's truck."

"Why did you do it Clay?"

"It was the only way I could keep my job." He glanced at Peter. "I don't have anything to fall back on, Peter. Old man Murphy always promised me that house and a little bit of money set aside for retirement. When he died and the will was read . . . nothing. All those years he lied to me."

"Did you kill Sam Geary?"

"No way, Peter! All I did was put those letters on his truck seat."

"Did Mr. Hayes ever threaten to harm Sam?"

"No. He thought those letters would scare Sam into moving the fence line. I knew they wouldn't, but I kept my mouth shut."

"All for a few feet of creek."

"Greed knows no bounds," commented Travis, as he led Clay to his jail cell.

Peter made his way to his office phone to begin the process of holding Winston Hayes accountable.

18

HIGH ON THE mountain in Peter's cozy cabin, Holly and John behaved with a misguided sense of security. They were certain not a soul beyond Peter knew where they were and trusted he would sacrifice his life before risking theirs. They played cribbage or worked jigsaw puzzles into the wee hours of the night and hiked familiar trails during the day, pausing to fish Peter's private lake for fresh trout dinner. They talked for hours about family and friends, and old times and new times to come. In turns, when they remembered to bring them, they would check the weapons at their belts or, in the evenings, glance at the twelve-gauge shotgun leaning against the door frame, assured that those tools would protect them against any invader. They were oblivious to the swiftness of a hidden enemy attacking from the woods or how quickly the cabin door could be kicked in. They were unaware of the watcher, who was also a tracker and had been watching them since the evening of their arrival. The watcher was aware of how easily they could be overcome and how useless were their weapons, forgotten across the room while they played their games. Even an inexperienced assailant could out gun them. So, the watcher watched and waited.

"Why didn't you ever tell me about our family legacy?" Holly asked John while they sat around the dying embers of a campfire, roasting marshmallows over the coals.

John pulled his roasting stick away from the heat and slipped the golden-brown crust off the marshmallow. He popped the crust into his mouth and thought while he chewed.

"There's so much money. So much land. I wanted to make sure you had a solid footing in life before you were handed that responsibility. You made it on your own without the money and found your passion. Even with all the wealth you just inherited, would you give up The Sapphire Pit?"

Holly thought about the money and land. The enormity of her inheritance was still beyond her comprehension, but she understood she could spend the rest of her life in luxury without working another day. But was The Sapphire Pit really work, or as her father said, 'her passion'?

"I love running The Sapphire Pit. I love teaching people about gems and rock formations and how the land was molded by time. Even with all the money I could ever want or need, I would keep doing what I love."

"I'm proud of you, Holly and your ancestors would be, too. You're the perfect person to carry on the family legacy . . . but . . ." he glanced up at her sheepishly.

"What, Dad?"

"You need to get married and have babies. We don't want the family legacy reverting to the likes of Bob Dahl and his stock."

Holly blushed.

"You and Peter going to work things out?"

A booming voice in the dark saved Holly from that awkward conversation.

"Hello at the camp."

They both jumped. John, at that moment realizing their vulnerability—the shotgun still leaning against the door frame in the cabin and both sidearms hanging on hooks inside the door—leaped to his feet in a fighting stance, ready to defend Holly. Out of the shadows came the figure of a large man, at first a stranger, and then familiar.

"Relax, brother John," said the voice. "I have yet to best you in a wrestling match."

Relieved almost to the point of tears, John held out his arms and embraced his younger brother, Alfred. The brothers held tight, years of separation to set right.

Remembering Holly, sitting in the shadows of the campfire, John pushed away from Alfred, turned toward Holly and asked, "Holly, do you remember your Uncle Alfred?"

"That's an interesting lantern you have there," laughed Alfred, following John's gaze.

Roasting stick clutched tightly in her hand, flaming marshmallow still dangling from the end, Holly stood poised to fend off an attacker. In her mind she had been imagining the many ways she could use the stick as a weapon. Shaking from the adrenaline racing through her body, she fumbled with the roasting stick, trying to anchor it between two fireside rocks, giving up and letting it fall to the ground. John saved her from her embarrassment by walking around the campfire and wrapping her in a giant bear hug.

"I haven't seen you since you were a bitty little cub, still clinging to your mama," said Alfred as he held her at arms-length and studied her face. "You're still not very big but have the heart of a grizzly bear judging by the way you were holding that marshmallow spear."

"Not much use against a grizzly or a guy with a gun," said Holly, aware of the rifle slung over his shoulder.

"Sometimes it's more about the fight than the firepower. Don't underestimate yourself."

"How did you find us, brother?" interrupted John. "We thought we were well disguised and well hid."

"You forget I make my living hunting and tracking. No worries, though. I've been watching for other trackers. Those mafia hunters aren't very effective outside the city."

"Are they still circling the block down there?"

"They were when I left town."

"We have a funeral to plan. We can't leave David lying down there."

"Only David's body is laying down there. It can wait. David is sitting at a coffee shop in heaven sipping strong black coffee and telling tall tales. You two need to stay here where you're safe until these Russians are under control."

"I know, 'funerals are for the living,' but we didn't get to say goodbye. We didn't have time to mourn."

"We're all hurting, John . . ." he broke off.

A quiet whimper came from the far side of the campfire. Holly, sitting on one of the old stumps they used for fireside chairs, head in hands, sobbed. The brothers glanced at each other and then back at Holly, helpless to know how to comfort her. In unspoken agreement, they left Holly to her mourning and busied themselves with the necessities of life.

"I brought extra supplies," said Alfred, turning and walking into the thick of trees and darkness where he had been hiding. He came back out pulling a bright blue all-terrain utility wagon.

John stifled a laugh watching the huge bear of a man pulling a wagon.

"I know, I know," said Alfred. "But it's easier than a heavy pack to drop if I get into a confrontation, and I can carry more stuff . . . including beer for you."

He pulled the wagon into the cabin and John helped him unload and store the supplies.

"Are we resigned to warm beer?" asked Alfred.

John grinned. "Grab that lantern and follow me."

He led Alfred around the back of the cabin and a short distance up the mountain on a well-traveled path. In the center of a small clearing stood a large rectangular cement tank, looking out of place amongst the trees and wildflowers. Someone had painted it with a mural of leaves and flowers in an attempt to make it look more a part of the wilderness but only managed to make it look like painted cement.

"What is that?"

"A cistern. Ice cold spring water flows in and then down to the cabin. It also functions as an incredible beer cooler, even in the hottest days of summer."

John slid the lid off the cistern and showed Alfred where shelves had been built to hold cold items.

"There's a filter between here and the cabin to catch any contamination."

"Cool!!!" Alfred grabbed a couple of already-chilled cans of beer. "Do you think Holly wants one?"

"Naw. She's not much of a beer drinker."

Safely tucked back in the cabin, the wood burning stove glowing red, Holly and John filled Alfred in on the details of David's murder.

"So, Peter is pretty sure the Russians hung David, but has no idea why he was poisoned first?"

"Nope. No clues where that pie came from or why," said John.

"Weird. He can't link it to the Russians?"

"It doesn't make sense. Especially after one of the thugs took a piece and poisoned himself."

"What?!"

"Oops. We forgot to tell you that part." John relayed the story of the thug found in the Clinton parking lot.

Holly, weary of rehashing the same conversations, said, "Uncle Alfred, tell us stories about big-game hunting in faraway lands."

And he did.

19

Funerals in a small town, especially unexpected deaths, touch the entire community. For a beloved community patriarch of David's caliber, all activity other than those relating to the funeral comes to a stop. Stores close in the middle of the day. Children are dismissed from school. Bank windows are shuttered. During winter months, finding a place large enough to accommodate in-town and surrounding area residents, and out-of-town relatives of the deceased presents a challenge. Most often those funerals are held in the school gymnasium unless the departed is particularly religious, then the funeral is held in the chosen church and overflow watches a live stream from the church hall.

Sam Geary, being a strict Mennonite, fell in a third category. His family chose a private burial in the family cemetery located in a high secluded meadow above the family home. A modest memorial service was scheduled after the burial for family and close friends.

"Should we send someone to Sam's memorial service today?" asked Travis as the crew sat at their morning donut and debriefing ritual.

"On the off chance his murderer shows up?" asked Tom.

"A long shot," said Peter, "but we should send someone to represent the sheriff's office. Helen?"

Helen sighed. "Sure. Token woman gets sent to do the touchy-feely stuff."

"You're just better at that stuff than the rest of us, except maybe Tom and he's not looking very presentable these days," said Peter eyeing Tom's black eyes and swollen nose framed by scratch marks down his cheeks. "Besides, we'll let you pick out the donuts tomorrow."

"I pick out, pick up, and bring in the donuts every morning."

"Yeah, but tomorrow we'll let you have first pick out of the box."

"Jerks! Where and when is the service?" asked Helen, resigned to her fate.

"Two. Community center. Thanks, Helen."

"Do I need to bring flowers or anything?"

"They're collecting for a memorial bench in the city park. Travis can give you some out of petty cash. Anything else exciting going on in town?"

"Brawl at the low-income housing units," said Travis. "Do you want me to send someone over to investigate?"

Peter rolled his eyes. "What now?"

"Tabitha Reynolds was blocking the sidewalk and wouldn't let anyone past."

"To hear my parents tell it," said Peter, "Tabitha's been a bully since the first day of preschool."

"She actually had a lawn chair out there waiting for victims. First one along was Jeremy, that autistic kid who just moved over from Nimrod. It was more than he could handle, and he turned tail and ran back to his apartment. She chased him, hurling insults the entire time," said Helen.

"Did she go inside his apartment?"

"No. She at least had sense enough to stop at the door."

"Dang. We could have gotten her on trespass. What next?"

"Then Bertha Hanson came along in her electric chair. She tried to avoid Tabitha by cutting across the lawn, but the grass was soaked because they had the sprinklers running all night."

"Wheelchair get stuck?"

"As stuck as four hundred pounds of Bertha sinking into wet grass can get," said Travis.

"Oh jeez. Did they get her out?"

"Had to call the fire department from Rumsey. They have a new bariatric lift. Four guys to lift her out and then unstick and clean off the chair. Our ambulance crew came over to give Bertha a once over."

"She okay?"

"Yeah. Just mad as a rabid chihuahua."

"And Tabitha sat and watched the whole thing?"

"Sipping iced tea and laughing the entire time. There was nothing we could do."

"I'm guessing it didn't end there."

"Here's the best part. Nancy May came along. She'd been watching the whole thing from the beginning and boy did she have her dander up," said Helen, chuckling at the memory.

"Oh boy."

"She started giving Tabitha a what for and Tabitha stood up and said, 'I'm going to knock your block off starting with that wig!' Nancy grabbed the wig right off her head and shoved it in Tabitha's face and said, 'Here. I'll make it easy on you.'"

Peter just about choked on his donut and Tom laughed so hard his face hurt. When they pulled themselves together, Peter asked, "How did Tabitha handle that?"

"The first time anyone's ever seen Tabitha speechless. She stood there with her mouth hanging open until Nancy told her to shut her trap and go to her room. Tabitha picked up her chair and went back to her apartment. I didn't think we needed to interfere since Nancy had it under control."

"Maybe we should hire her for domestic calls."

"Oh boy, wouldn't that be a hoot!"

They sipped their tea and coffee and contemplated seventy-five-year-old Nancy May in a deputy uniform.

"On a more serious note, did we check Barb and Bob for rabies?" asked Tom, patting his tender cheek.

"They're still in custody and refusing to talk. They already spent every cent of the Russian money so don't have the funds to bail themselves out," said Peter.

"What about the son?"

Travis laughed. "He called and said it was their policy when he was growing up that if he ever ended up in jail, he could just sit there and serve his time because they weren't going to bail him out. So, he said he was going to follow the good lessons they taught him and let them sit here and serve their time."

"Not a loving relationship then."

"Nope. In words I won't repeat, he was very specific that they were not to call him, and he wanted nothing to do with any of their issues."

"Do you think he's complicit and trying to distance himself?" asked Peter.

"He didn't seem overly concerned about his parents when I talked to him in Missoula," said Helen. "It was like Travis said, he was annoyed. After years of dealing with them, he's done."

"Okay, we won't waste time in that direction for now. Did Bob and Barb get a lawyer?"

"Public defender," said Travis.

"Harold?"

"Yeah."

"Good luck with that one."

Harold Erickson's exact age was not known, but judging by looks, he was a close friend of Moses. Although his methods and results were questionable, as long as he continued to take the most undesirable cases, no one was rushing to push him out.

"Boss."

"Yeah, Travis."

"Word around town is there are a couple guys hanging out at Dixie's café every afternoon."

"Causing trouble?"

"No. They have lunch and then sit there and drink a couple gallons of coffee and eat pie."

"So. What's the problem?" asked Peter, wondering how many hours of his life he had spent dragging conversation points out of people.

"They're obviously not locals and Dixie thinks they're trying hard to look like tourists, but don't have a clue. You know, pastel plaid shorts on legs that have never seen the sun, black dress socks with sandals."

"Does Dixie have any more thoughts I should know about?"

"She thinks they're Russians, but they don't have an accent."

"Some of the Russians we're looking for are from Washington State. They were probably born here," said Helen.

"Does anyone in town not know about the Russian issue?" asked Peter.

Tom snorted. "Not likely."

"Dixie sees a lot of people. She's a good judge," said Travis. "I think we should check them out."

"Okay," said Peter. "I'll go over for lunch. Anyone like to join me?"

Three hands shot up. "Noon-thirty at Dixie's then."

"I'll call and have her save us a table," said Travis.

All three were seated and eagerly scanning menus when Peter walked into Dixie's café. He hung his hat and coat at the door and, as casually as possible, scanned the room for the reported Russians. At the back corner table, sticking out like cats in a dog show, were the two guys. Travis's description was spot on down to the black dress socks and Birkenstock sandals. *In the back facing the door so they can see everyone coming in,* thought Peter. *I wonder who they're watching for?* Then he realized why his employees were there early. They saved him the seat facing the alleged Russians, but the deputy who showed up last, Tom, had to take the seat facing away. He sat with a scowl on his face.

"Did I miss anything?" asked Peter.

"Not yet," said Travis. "We were hoping you would stir things up."

Peter glanced at the back table. The two men glared at him and his deputies.

"I don't think they like us," commented Helen.

To prove her point, the balding and beefy guy on the right looked straight at Peter and swept his arm across the table, knocking what was left of their lunch, plates and all, to the floor.

Was that a dare? thought Peter.

A flustered waitress hurried out with a tray to pick up the mess. Dixie followed her with a broom and dustpan. Mr. Beefy sat staring at Peter with a smirk on his face while his equally beefy partner, sporting a full set of hair and a nose swollen and veined from years of drink, lobbed insults at the waitress, calling her stupid and clumsy when she bent to add more shards to her tray and it tipped, several pieces landing on his sandaled foot.

"That's it!" said Peter. Three strides of his long legs brought him to the edge of the back table, his deputies at his flank. "First, you are going to apologize to Dixie and this waitress."

Mr. Beefy, still with the smirk. "So sorry, officer. It was a simple accident."

"It was no accident. You will apologize to these ladies and then you are under arrest for willful destruction of property."

Four eyes filled with menace met Peter's stony gaze. The men wrestled their collective bulk out from the booth, a task they were unable to achieve with dignity. Beefy, obviously the spokesman, said, "You don't know who you're dealing with."

"I have a pretty good idea. Apologize."

"So sorry, miss," said The Schnoz, eyes never leaving Peter.

"Turn around and place your hands behind your back," said Peter.

The Schnoz looked at Beefy for guidance. Beefy scanned the room. Behind Peter and his deputies stood a mob of angry townspeople, all armed and ready for a fight. Beefy relented and turned. The Schnoz followed suit. Both were too large for handcuffs, so Helen pulled zip ties out of her utility belt and quickly secured the men.

"You'll regret this," said Beefy, still with the smirk.

"I doubt it," said Peter, hand on his shoulder, guiding him toward the exit. As they reached the door, Peter glanced at the corner table. Mavis Vallee was writing furiously in a notebook. *I guess I don't need to give her a statement,* thought Peter.

Crisis diverted, the diners were back at their plates, chewing fries and chatting like nothing had happened.

Beefy was loaded into Peter's vehicle and The Schnoz into Tom's. Helen stayed back and took witness statements. The general public was thrilled to have 'those foreign thugs' off the streets.

During the booking process, Peter wasn't surprised to find that neither man carried identification. They were fingerprinted and given orange jumpsuits and locked into separate cells. Both men refused to speak. Neither asked for a lawyer or desired a phone call. Peter informed them individually that it would be a good idea to call their boss. He wanted a face-to-face conversation with whoever was behind the murders and intimidation.

"Do you think there are more of them in town?" asked Travis when they were back in the office.

"We can't assume anything. The fact that neither one has tried to make a phone call worries me."

The reality was both Beefy and The Schnoz knew they screwed up by getting arrested. When their boss, who was a few layers down the food chain from the big boss, found out they had drawn attention to themselves by antagonizing the local sheriff, they were sure to be eliminated.

Beefy quickly went through his options. Ratting out his bosses wasn't an option. When they caught up with him . . . and they would catch up with him . . . they would torture him before they killed him. He knew. He was the one they sent out to hunt down and torture rats. Or used to be. His only option was to escape before his bosses found out.

The Schnoz answered to Beefy. He was more brawn than brains and being eliminated hadn't crossed his mind. His number one concern was how to get a drink. He knew from experience that after too many hours in a holding cell without alcohol, he would go into DTs and that scared him more than a mad boss.

Later, when Travis brought by a tray of dinner, The Schnoz slapped on the closest thing he had to a charming smile.

"Hey, buddy. This looks great. Is there any chance I could get a beer to wash this down?"

Travis took a close look at The Schnoz. He registered the swollen veined nose of a chronic alcoholic.

"I'll talk to the sheriff."

Travis took the steps to the sheriff's office two at a time. A desperate alcoholic was just the leverage they needed. He picked up the phone and punched in Peter's number, praying he hadn't decided to hike to the cabin to check on Holly and John.

Peter, who had been sitting on the back deck at his brother Paul's house enjoying a Cold Smoke, looked at his cell phone and saw that the call was coming through from the sheriff's office.

"This is Peter."

"Hey, Boss, guess what."

Peter sighed. "I have no idea, Travis. Just tell me."

"The thug, the one with the big nose, he all but begged me for a drink."

"He's an alcoholic. Probably too early to worry about DTs. We can't give him booze."

"He might spill the beans and call his boss if we offer to let him out. He can get his own booze."

"Good point. Call Doc. I want him to check the guy out and be there while we question him. I'll call the county attorney and make sure we're not crossing any legal lines. Travis?"

"Yeah, Boss?"

"Good work."

SUBDUED BECAUSE HE had been promised a possible release, The Schnoz submitted to Dr. Hamm's examination. He also acknowledged his legal name, Bernard Eugene Smirnov, but asked to be called Bernie.

"His blood pressure's slightly high and he's sweating, but those symptoms may be normal for him. He's an overweight alcoholic. I am worried about the slight tremor in his hands. They may be the beginnings of DTs. I'll stay and monitor him, but my advice is to finish your questioning and get him out of here as soon as possible."

"Thanks, Doc," said Peter. They were sitting in Peter's office, both longing for an early release as much as the prisoner.

"I suggest you leave him in a cell while you question him, though. Ongoing DT symptoms could include irritability and anxiety."

"Travis, let's move Bernie to the holding cell up here," said Peter as he stood, grabbed his hat, and whistled for Zack. People often told him the cowboy hat gave him an air of authority and Zack's friendly manner tended to sooth even the most cantankerous prisoner.

Cooperation wasn't a problem with Bernie. He was planning his first drink and would do nothing to risk losing that freedom. He gave them every name, date, and place he knew including Beefy, who he knew only as Ivanov, no last name. He confirmed that he and Ivanov worked for the Russian mafia out of Washington State. They were sent to town with pictures of Holly, Bob, and Barb and orders to eliminate. He didn't know why. He wasn't that far up in the chain of command. Finally, Peter handed Bernie the telephone and instructed him to call the only number he knew, the one he called to receive orders and report results.

"Tell them I have the information they need. They'll get nowhere killing those people. Tell them I need to talk to whoever is in charge, not some underling."

Bernie made the call, relayed the message, and gave Peter's cell phone number to whoever was on the other end of the line. The voice didn't sound friendly, but Bernie was oblivious. The voice said he would pass along the message.

"Can I go now?" asked Bernie eagerly.

Peter glanced at Doc. "What do you think?"

"Medically he is doing fine. I see no reason not to release him."

"You understand, Bernie," said Peter "that your orders to kill those people are null and void?"

"Null and void?" asked Bernie with a blank look.

"Your orders have been cancelled. If we let you go you need to promise us you will leave town and never come back."

"After I have a drink?"

Peter sighed. "We don't want you driving out of town drunk. You can stay in town tonight and leave tomorrow. Sober. One of our deputies will escort you out of town.

"Wow! A police escort. Wait 'till I tell the guys!"

Travis stifled a laugh and Doc rolled his eyes. Peter nodded to Travis, who stood and unlocked the cell door with keys from his utility belt. He grabbed the pile of Bernie's clothes off his desk, along with a bag of personal belongings, minus a gun and car keys, and led Bernie into the bathroom to change.

"Do you think the mafia will *eliminate* him?" asked Doc.

"Probably. Not our problem," said Peter. "Live by the gun, die by the gun and all that. Remember, he's a cold-blooded killer. He didn't kill Holly and the Dahls, but he would have."

"Why are we letting him go?"

"We have nothing to hold him on. Dixie isn't going to press charges. His fingerprints may come back with a hit, but we don't have time to wait, and we need the contact with his bosses so we can get rid of them for good."

"I guess you know what you're doing," said Doc, as he waved goodbye and headed out the door.

"Thanks, Doc. We owe you one."

Travis and Bernie were out of the bathroom, Bernie back in his street clothes.

"We'll take my Explorer," said Peter.

He had a specially-designed vehicle with the back seat separated into two compartments; one for a prisoner and one for a police dog, Zack. Peter and Travis led Bernie down the back stairs and loaded him and Zack into the back of Peter's Explorer.

"Did you and Ivanov come in separate vehicles?" asked Peter.

"Yeah, we met up here."

When they drove past the café, Bernie pointed out his car, a late-model Cadillac.

"We need to search your car before we let you go. Do you have a problem with that?"

"Aww, man."

"Sorry, buddy. Part of the deal."

"I still get to leave, right?"

"No matter what we find, deal is still on."

"Yeah, sure," said Bernie, doubtfully.

The Cadillac was immaculate, which made the search easier.

"Who would've thought a thug like that would be a neatnik?" said Travis.

"He loves his car."

The search turned up three guns, all with serial numbers filed off: a 9mm in the glove box and an AK47 and 30-06 with a scope in the trunk.

Travis tagged and bagged the guns and locked them in the evidence locker in Peter's vehicle.

"Okay, Bernie. We found and confiscated three guns. Is there anything else you want to declare before we let you go?"

"Naw, that's all."

"Are you sure? Anything that might be found after this won't be part of the deal."

"Honest. That's all. Those three guns."

Peter opened the door and watched as Bernie maneuvered his bulk to the ground. He handed him his car keys.

"You guys staying at the Sapphire Inn?"

"Yeah."

"Straight to the grocery store for whatever you need and then to your room. We'll follow and make sure you don't get lost."

"Yeah, yeah," said Bernie as he shuffled to his car.

Back in his own vehicle, Peter phoned Helen and apprised her of the situation.

"Watch this guy but keep undercover. Keep me posted."

"Sure, Boss," sighed Helen, not looking forward to a long night of surveillance.

Coming out of the grocery store, Bernie made a show of holding up a case of beer and two bottles of wine, his only options after five. Peter followed and watched him key himself into his room at the inn. They waited until Helen pulled up in one of the county's unmarked cars, gave her a wave and drove back to drop Travis off in his car.

A SHRILL RINGING pulled Peter out of a deep sleep. It never got easier.

"Yeah, this is Peter."

"We got him," said Helen.

"Who? What's going on," asked Peter, still groggy.

"Bernie. The thug. He stumbled out of his room about half an hour ago dragging his suitcase. It fell open and his clothes are strung out across the parking lot."

Wide awake now, Peter asked. "He tried to make a run for it?"

"Yeah. I let him get into the car and start it up before I pulled up behind him with my lights going. He's so drunk he would have backed right into me if I hadn't hit the siren. Of course, the motel manager is mad because I woke up the other guests."

"Tell her to charge extra for the Wild West show. Where is he now?"

"Zip tied and on his butt in the parking lot."

"He give you trouble?"

"Yeah, but I tased him. There's no way I'm getting him into the car by myself."

"Call the ambulance crew and let them know you have a large load. I'll be right down."

The Stone County ambulance crew included several strong ranch boys who grew up steer wrestling at home and in the rodeo. As they informed Peter afterwards, wrestling one passed out Russian thug was a piece of cake compared to a mad cow.

"What are you going to do about this room, Peter?" demanded an angry Cora Hanson.

The room was a shambles. Empty beers cans littered the floor. Both wine bottles were smashed against the wall, wine dripping down and staining the wall and carpets, cigarette butts crushed out on every available surface. Peter refused to go into the bathroom. The stench told the story.

"The sheriff's department is not responsible for this mess, Cora. You can press charges for destruction of property. Call your insurance company."

"But you brought him here. I saw you."

"Uh, no. He drove himself here because he had a room rented here, that you rented to him. We followed him to make sure he didn't leave town."

"And that deputy of yours, Helen, has been sitting out here all night. How do you explain that?"

"She was watching to make sure he didn't leave town. If she hadn't been here, who knows how many cars he would have hit trying to get out of the parking lot. Your guests would have really been mad then."

"As it is, half of them are demanding their money back."

"I'm sorry, Cora. I really am, but this is not the first time we've been here arresting a drunk who smashed up a room. It happens every rodeo, class reunion, family reunion, Fourth of July . . ."

Cora glared at him, turned and stomped back to her office apartment.

***

"THE HOSPITAL IS going to keep him until he's detoxed," said Travis the next morning as they gathered for their morning debriefing.

"Did anything come back on those fingerprints?" asked Peter.

"Oh, yeah. Both these thugs are wanted for a laundry list of crimes ranging from petty theft to murder."

"Washington State?"

"Multiple states, but mostly in Washington. Several murders there."

"Good. Contact the police chief or sheriff or whoever is looking for these guys and we'll get them shipped out as soon as possible. I don't want to deplete our county budget detoxing Bernie."

"What about the mob contact?"

"We've already made contact. Shipping these guys out shouldn't make a difference."

Peter's phone pinged. An unlisted number.

"Speak of the devil," he said as he swiped to answer and put his finger to his lips to silence his staff.

"This is Peter Elliott."

"Mr. Elliott," said a smooth, surprisingly-cultured voice. "I have a message to contact you about a business venture. I hope you understand if I don't share my name."

"No problem. I'm most interested in clearing up confusion about land ownership in my county."

"Understandable. I will be in touch." And then the connection was broken.

"Even if we were trying to trace that call on a land line, it wasn't long enough," said Helen.

"It's a start," said Peter. "At least we know he got the message."

"Any chance we can send Bob and Barb with them?" asked Travis. "Those two are the most whiney, entitled prisoners we've ever had. Barb actually asked if she could go to her quilting group in Nimrod today and accused me of discrimination and abuse when I said no."

"I wish, but we're stuck with them. At least until they go to court. Even then, resisting arrest and assault on a police officer will keep them here in jail."

"Oh, yeah," said Helen, remembering the rolled newspaper she had in her hand. "Did you see this week's *Chronicle*?"

She handed the paper to Peter, who unrolled and smoothed it on his desk.

"Murderer Remains at Large," declared the head-line. *Person or persons responsible for the cruel poisoning of local patriarch, David Howard, remain free in our community. Are any of us safe? Who will be the next victim?*

"Good grief," said Peter. "Have we had any calls from panicked citizens?"

"Not yet," said Travis, "but it's early yet."

Peter spent the rest of the day reading and dozing in his office. Or staring into space. With all the Dahls accounted for, either in jail or protective custody, and Holly and John safely hidden at the cabin, his main concern was the mafia boss. He doubted any legitimate mafia boss would have a phone conversation that could be taped or traced. Would he agree to meet with Peter? Would he listen to reason if he did? Was he, Peter, in danger? The day was unusually quiet in spite of Mavis's inciting article, as if the entire community sensed danger and stayed safely at home. Peter left his office early, watching for a tail all the way. He double checked the locks on doors and windows. People in Anderson didn't have electronic security systems, they had four legged ones. He hoped Zack would be enough.

⸻•◦•◦•◦•⸻

THREE A.M. AND a shrill clanging pulled Peter out of an unusually pleasant dream. Irritated, he grabbed his phone from the bedside table and snapped "What now?!" at the caller.

"Mr. Elliott. That is not a respectful manner to greet an associate."

The Russian.

Peter, now wide awake, said, "My apologies. As with most people, I was asleep at three a.m."

"And my apologies to you. My business keeps me up at odd hours. I forget at times that they are not traditional working hours."

I'll bet, thought Peter. *All a ploy to catch me alone and off guard and make sure it's a cell phone and not a land line.* "Why did you call?" he asked.

"You desired a meeting. I would like to arrange a time and place."

Peter had already thought this out. "Smitty's Pancake House. Missoula. Ten a.m. tomorrow. Your *associates* should be familiar with the location."

"I usually conduct business meetings in quieter, less public venues."

"This isn't a business meeting. I have information that you need. If I'm going to meet a stranger with questionable motives, I'd rather be in a public place."

Silence.

"Ten a.m. tomorrow. You alone. I am also trusting you to keep this meeting confidential."

"See you tomorrow," said Peter as he disconnected.

What the mobster didn't know was that Smitty's Pancake House was also a popular hangout of the local police force. The owner's son, Pinky, was a twenty-year veteran and head detective in the force. Law enforcement was given a significant discount. Any time of day there was likely to be several officers, in and out of uniform, scattered amongst the patrons. And then there was Layla, the hostess. Peter was in safe hands.

20

NOT THE HIGHEST-RANKING member of the organization, but high enough to be accustomed to deference, respect, and definitely fear, Dimitri Volkov was not prepared for Layla. Strong and fit from years of wrestling wayward calves and bucking bales of hay, combined with the stick straight straw-colored hair most often associated with hardy Scandinavian women, Layla was an imposing figure and had the personality to match. She sized up Dimitri as a self-important thug when he strode in the door of Smitty's Pancake House and resolved to knock him down a peg or two before he had a chance to cause trouble.

"Do you have reservations?" she asked, although Smitty's had not required reservations in the entire thirty years the restaurant had been open.

Dimitri bristled. "I do not need reservations. I have a business meeting. Give me a quiet table in back," he demanded.

"All we have available are stools at the counter," lied Layla, and that is where she led him.

Dimitri fought the urge to walk out. He was insulted and humiliated sitting at the counter in his Brioni suit, the brand he wore because it was preferred by James Bond, and he imagined himself the James Bond of the Russian Mafia. Bond would not be sitting at a counter stool in a pancake house. But Dimitri was not at the top of the food chain, and he had orders. He had orders to meet with the Stone County sheriff and listen to what he had to say. Dimitri may have been higher up in command than Bernie, but he, too, was expendable.

There was an empty stool next to Dimitri. A middle-aged farmer wearing faded and dirty overalls tried to sit down. Dimitri put his hand on the stool and said, "No!" The farmer shrugged and took a stool at the end of the row, returning to Dimitri a smidgeon of his dignity.

Peter was sitting in his Explorer in the parking lot when Dimitri walked into Smitty's. Like Layla, he pegged Dimitri for a mafia boss as soon as he saw him in that fancy suit. Not many people in Missoula would be wearing a suit like that and they wouldn't be wearing it to Smitty's. In his own power play, Peter waited ten minutes before he walked into the building.

Layla greeted him with a smile. "Hi, Peter. I have your table clean and waiting for you."

"The suit that just walked in. Could you let him know I'm here and he can join me at my table?"

Layla wrinkled her nose in disgust. "You used to be more particular who you hung out with."

"He's not a friend," said Peter. "It's work."

Layla watched Peter walk to his usual table, but waited for a good ten minutes, enjoying the obvious discomfort of Dimitri on his bar stool.

After she finally led him to Peter's table and left, Dimitri said, "Why do you get a table? I was told they were unavailable."

"Certain tables are kept free for preferred customers," Peter said casually.

Frustrated, Dimitri said, "You are late. That is poor business."

"I told you this isn't a business meeting."

"Then tell me this important information so I can get out of here."

"I'm assuming you're not the head of the organization?"

"No," admitted Dimitri. "But I have great power."

"I doubt it," said Peter, "or you wouldn't be here."

Dimitri glared at him.

"Do you need to take notes, or can you remember this?" asked Peter, wondering if he was pushing Dimitri too far. But he, unlike Dimitri, was facing the dining room. He could see the eyes and the slow nods of the other law enforcement in the room. They knew something was going down and they had his back.

Dimitri continued to glare.

Peter relented. "Tell whoever you answer to that no matter how many people are murdered, threatened, or bribed, there is no way your organization will ever gain control of the land around Anderson. It is permanently tied up in legal trusts that can't be broken. I know your bosses already have a copy of the will of Charles Anderson and used that to track down heirs."

Peter handed him a copy of an addendum to the will of Charles Anderson that had been found in David's house. It stated that in the event no heirs to the Anderson fortune existed, then control of the land and monies would pass to Stone County to be held in perpetuity with the same rules of ownership applying.

"We know the thug who murdered David Howard and Sam Geary is dead along with another couple of thugs who tried to murder Robert and Anne Marie

Dahl. We have Ivanov and Bernie in custody under separate charges. Bob and Barb Dahl are in custody and won't be getting out any time soon. You promise to leave Stone County and never come back, and we'll let things go with that."

Dimitri studied the paper with an interest and understanding that made Peter think he had underestimated the ranking of this well-dressed man in the Russian organization.

Dimitri nodded and looked up at Peter, holding his gaze. "Agreed," he said and, in an uncharacteristic show of candor, held out his hand. As they shook to seal the deal, Dimitri said, "Well played, Sheriff, well played."

Dimitri stood and walked toward the entrance, forced to pass Layla at her hostess podium.

"Call ahead next time and I'll save your bar stool," she said.

"Never again," he muttered.

21

D EW WAS HEAVY along the game trail leading away from Anderson and into the mountain trees. The early morning sun was enough to bring light and warmth to the earth, but not enough to keep Peter's socks dry, hence the extra pair in his pack. He slept soundly the night before, all threats of Russians and murder gone from his mind.

His staff had asked, in disbelief, "Do you really think we can trust these guys?" "Yes," he'd replied.

Zack chased squirrels and rabbits and birds, running circles around Peter on their way up the mountain to tell Holly and John it was safe to come home. At the edge of the tree line, Peter stopped, turned, and studied the valley below, imagining the lush green meadows and free-flowing Flint Creek replaced with resort hotels and swimming pools. Pine trees cut down to make way for parking lots and tennis courts. He silently thanked Charles Anderson for his wisdom all those ages ago.

In front of the fire pit, setting a match to kindling and paper, Peter saw an unfamiliar figure and his heart skipped a beat. Zack growled, but obediently stayed by Peter's side. The man was tall and well-built, and Peter was glad he was armed. He reached for his gun and loudly advised the man to stand, turn around, and put his hands in the air. To Peter's surprise, the man not only complied, but did so with a friendly smile.

"You must be Peter."

"Yes. I own this cabin. Who are you?"

Holly came around the corner carrying a Styrofoam carton of eggs and a tub of bacon from the cistern. John was following with a bottle of orange juice.

When Zack saw Holly, his tail wagged so hard his whole backend swayed back and forth.

"Peter!" Holly exclaimed. "What are you doing with that gun?"

"I came to bring you two home and found this strange man by the fire. Do you know him?"

"This is my brother, Alfred," laughed John. "Holly's uncle."

Peter lowered his gun and replaced it in his holster. "How did you get here?" he asked.

"Uncle Alfred is a hunter and tracker," said Holly. "There's nothing he can't track, including a couple of doofuses like us in goofy costumes."

"When John told me David was murdered and the whole family was in danger, I came as soon as I could, but didn't let anyone know I was here. Protecting from afar seemed like the best way to help until I knew John and Holly were safe here at your cabin."

"Take a load off, Peter," said John. "Alfred is a master chef when it comes to campfire cooking."

While Alfred cooked, Peter filled everyone in on everything that had happened while they were gone.

"Do you really think you can trust those guys to stay away?" asked Alfred with the same tone of disbelief as Peter's staff.

"Yeah," said Peter. "When the guy I met with saw the papers and realized no amount of bullying would get them what they wanted, he shook my hand and walked away."

"Gosh," said Holly. "I was having so much fun camping with Dad and Uncle Alfred, I'm kind of disappointed that we have to go home."

"All of you are welcome to stay as long as you want," offered Peter.

"Holly," said John, suddenly somber, "we have a funeral to plan."

With that the four of them pitched in to clean up the breakfast mess. Holly, John, and Alfred packed their things. A quiet and reflective group made their way down the trail to town.

22

WHERE THERE ARE people, there is death and a multitude of rituals for dealing with the resulting bodies. Ancient Egyptians turned their loved ones into mummies, Tibetan monks left bodies to be consumed by scavengers in sky burials. Death rituals of the early inhabitants of Anderson were not quite so exotic. Graves were dug, caskets lowered, prayers said, and hymns sung, but only if women, children, and a pastor were present. Men left alone were satisfied with wrapping the body of a friend in a blanket before gifting it to the grave. Enemies didn't warrant wasting a blanket.

Lacking a pastoral meadow overlooking the valley, and not wanting to establish a cemetery in the waterlogged creek bed below, Andersonites buried their dead amongst the pine and fir of an east facing slope, wherever a space occurred large enough to accommodate a grave. Some were deeper than others depending on the number and size of underground rocks and roots and the ambition of the gravedigger.

Families adapted. Plots wound around trees and boulders, wrought iron fences taking the shape of the terrain. The best plots were first come, first served, with very few clamoring to be first in line.

David Howard was buried there, next to ancestors and strangers, but all sharing a kinship with the settlement below. In traditional Anderson fashion, the funeral service was conducted under the trees, alongside the newly-dug grave. Mourners sat on tombstones and leaned against trees, formality not a priority for the hardworking folks in an unrefined Montana mining town. Only when a sprinkle of rain became a torrent did they acknowledge vulnerability and make their way down the mountain, leaving a few stragglers to fill the hole.

Later that evening, Angus sat at the back corner table in the brewery, sipping his favorite pale ale and contemplating life. He missed Holly. A quick hug and "sorry for your loss" were all he managed at the funeral before she was whisked away by others. Peter was also prominent, but he and Holly weren't obviously a couple.

A group of local party girls came in and sat at the table next to him. They'd been drinking hard at the funeral, whiskey flasks shamelessly passed back and forth, leaving to bar hop when the rain hit. A designated driver wasn't obvious, but maybe they were walking or taking a cab home. Angus decided to pay attention and save them and everyone else on the road from a tragic accident. Liz Benton was the ringleader, and he was just as happy they didn't see him sitting in the dark corner. She was known to be a mean drunk and could be ruthless when she spotted a target.

"Maybe they were waiting until after the funeral to arrest her," said a girl in a tight leather skirt and way too much makeup.

"I heard she was in protective custody because of that Russian stuff, but maybe she was really in jail in another town," said another friend hopefully, the neck of her blood-red blouse cut provocatively low.

"Peter would try and protect her precious reputation," said Liz bitterly. "He can only protect her for so long though."

"You could call in an anonymous tip," suggested leather skirt, flipping her bleached blonde hair.

"What would I say?" asked a sneering Liz. "I forged a note with Holly's name and put it on a poisoned pie. Why haven't you arrested her yet?"

"I heard they have Bob Dahl in jail. What if he rats on you?" asked a third girl, in a belly shirt and low-cut jeans, a butterfly tramp stamp peeking out at Angus between the chair rails.

"If he rats on me, he rats on himself. He knew what he was doing when he baked that pie."

The girls went silent as a waitress approached their table. "Another round?" she asked.

They all ordered. Angus had heard enough and knew the girls wouldn't be going anywhere soon. He snuck out the back door, called Peter and filled him in on everything he'd heard.

"Go back in and keep your eye on them. Don't let them leave. We'll be there as soon as we can."

Peter walked through the front door fifteen minutes later and went straight to the back table where Liz Benton and her friends sat. Helen came through the back door.

"Peter!" slurred a drunk Liz. "I'm so glad you're here. Come sit next to me sweety."

"You can have my chair," said Tramp Stamp, as she slid over to make room.

Peter and Helen looked at each other in disbelief. They each pulled out two sets of handcuffs.

"Kind of early for cuffs, isn't it?" said Leather Skirt, with a wink.

"You are all under arrest for conspiracy to commit murder," said Peter snapping one set of cuffs around Liz's wrist, while Helen cuffed Tramp Stamp and read them their rights. Liz went nuts.

"I did it for you, Peter. You don't deserve my love," she screamed and then spit in his face.

Tramp Stamp started to cry, claiming everyone else forced her to go along. Helen caught Red Blouse trying to sneak out the back, while Leather Skirt crawled under the adjoining table, stopped by Zack who was on guard duty. Angus, still on crutches, wasn't much help, but by then the rest of the bar was involved. Liz and her buddies were not well liked. Red Blouse and Leather Skirt were placed under citizen's arrest several times over by enthusiastic drunks and held until Peter could get to them.

When the four women were secured in patrol cars, Peter said to Angus, "Call your Uncle Jake and ask if we can rent some space in his jail. We haven't had this many prisoners since that biker gang came through and tore things up."

Angus made the call. Jake agreed. Since Peter could only haul one prisoner in his vehicle, he called Tom in to transport two women to Rumsey, while Helen took the other two. Helen debated whether listening to the verbal abuse of a drunken Liz Benton was worse than enduring the Dahls fight during their transport. It was a toss-up.

⸺•••◦•••⸺

"SO, LIZ'S FRIENDS spilled the beans?" asked Travis, as the crew sat around his desk in their morning briefing.

"They didn't even ask for lawyers. They seemed to think that since they had only helped Liz pick the berries, they weren't complicit," said Peter.

"Mavis is hounding us for the whole story."

"Go ahead and give it to her. Let's get an accurate story out there before the Missoula papers run with it."

Later that day, Peter was at the kitchen table, eating oatmeal raisin cookies and filling Paul and Linda in on the end of the case.

"Liz tried to blame Bob Dahl to get herself out of trouble," said Peter. "They were out on the deck one day and Bob was reading that book you saw in their house about cooking with poisonous plants. Liz was complaining to Bob because she decided I was going to marry her."

"Marry you?" laughed Paul. "I didn't know you were close."

"We're not. It was news to me. Anyway, she got this idea in her head that she was going to marry me, but Holly was in the way. Bob was complaining about David getting in the way of his land deal. Between the two of them and a whole lot of alcohol, they concocted this plan to get rid of both Holly and David. Liz recognized the deadly nightshade from pictures in the book. She knew about a huge patch of it out by the old gravel pit."

"I remember," said Paul. "We rode our bikes out there when we were kids and mom always warned us not to eat the poisonous berries."

"It used to be a popular spot for high schoolers to hold keggers, too, until we started patrolling on a regular basis. That's probably where Liz began her drinking career. Anyway, she knew about the berries and convinced these three friends to go out and help her pick enough for a pie. Bob baked it. Liz forged the note and brought it to David. He died before he could tell anyone who delivered it.

"And Barb didn't know anything about it?" asked Linda.

"No. She was at a quilting show that day. By the time she got back the deed was done and so much attention was focused on David's death by hanging, Bob and Liz thought they were off the hook."

"Then why did Barb help Bob hide and fight so hard when you found them?" asked Paul.

"She thought he was in trouble for making a deal with the Russians. That's what he told her. In reality, there's nothing illegal about getting a personal loan from anyone. She'll still have to face the charges of resisting arrest and assaulting a police officer."

"Will Bob, Liz, and her friends be charged with murder?"

"I'm not sure. They'll be charged with attempted murder. If David hadn't been hanged, he would have died from the poisoning, but the autopsy ruled death by strangulation as a result of the hanging even though he was already passed out from the poison. The county attorney will have to decide if they are guilty of murder as well."

"And Winston Hayes?"

"He's in the clear. He admitted he wrote the threatening notes to Sam but has proof he hasn't been out of Connecticut since he originally came to inspect his new land purchase. Sam was in the wrong place at the wrong time. The mafia thugs thought they were killing Bob."

"I'm bummed I didn't get a chance to help more," said Linda. "How many more murders could possibly happen in this little town?"

Hopefully none, thought Peter.

Home again in the peaceful quiet of his den, Peter settled into his easy chair and pondered the manilla envelope lying on a chairside table. He picked it up and read the label. *Missoula County Sheriff's Office. Homicide. Elliott.* He fingered the clasp and thought about his parents. Remembering how they looked was easy, he had pictures. Voices, scent, touch, those were harder. As the years slipped by, the memories became hazier. He sighed. His parents' murder, the event that led him into law enforcement. All these years later he couldn't bring himself to open the envelope containing the murder notes. And murder pictures. There it was. He couldn't bear to see the graphic images of his parents' bodies after their murder, to read the details. How many years, how hazy the details before he would be able to investigate and bring them justice? The envelope, returned unopened to its resting place, haunted his dreams. He popped the top on a can of Cold Smoke, clicked on the television, and tried to forget.

Thank you for
reading Land Grab!

Have you considered leaving
a review? Reviews help me
spread the word and help other
readers decide if they want
to enjoy the book, too.

Please scan the QR code
below and let me know
what you think! :)

-Kit

GET YOUR FREE EBOOK

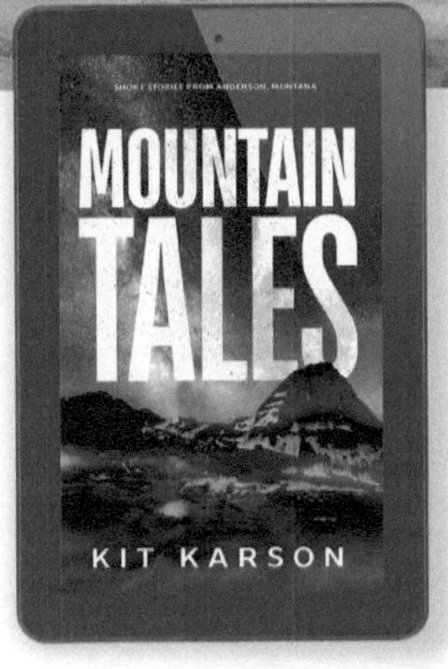

Join the citizens of Anderson in *Mountain Tales,* an ever-growing collection of short stories about past and present mysteries.

SIGN UP AT KITKARSON.COM

BOOK 2 IS HERE

A young woman goes missing, and she's not the first. Join Sheriff Elliott and new deputies as they race against the clock to find her before it's too late.

FIND IT AT KITKARSON.COM/BOOKS